Fabulous Fathers

"Daniel wants you to be his mother,"

Jess began.

The very thought of it made Hannah want to cry and smile at the same time. "I feel honored that he does. But you and I both know that it's impossible for me to be his mother."

"Why is that?"

"Because I didn't give birth to him."

"It takes more than giving birth to be a mother," Jess said gruffly. Then he sighed and added in a gentler tone, "And you could be Daniel's stepmother."

It took a moment for his words to sink in. When they did, Hannah began to tremble all over.

"What . . . are you saying?"

Shoving his hand through his hair, Jess glanced out the window. "I'm saying that—" He took a deep breath. "I'm telling you that I want you to marry me."

Dear Reader,

Welcome to the fourth great month of CELEBRATION 1000! We're winding up this special event with fireworks!— six more dazzling love stories that will light up your summer nights. The festivities begin with *Impromptu Bride* by beloved author Annette Broadrick. While running for their lives, Graham Douglas and Katie Kincaid had to marry. But will their hasty wedding lead to everlasting love?

Favorite author Elizabeth August will keep you enthralled with *The Forgotten Husband*. Amnesia keeps Eloise from knowing the real reason she'd married rugged, brooding Jonah Tavish. But brief memories of sweet passion keep her searching for the truth.

This month our FABULOUS FATHER is *Daniel's Daddy*— a heartwarming story by Stella Bagwell.

Debut author Kate Thomas brings us a tale of courtship— Texas-style in—*The Texas Touch*.

There's love and laughter when a runaway heiress plays *Stand-in Mom* in Susan Meier's romantic romp. And don't miss Jodi O'Donnell's emotional story of a love all but forgotten in *A Man To Remember*.

We'd love to know if you have enjoyed CELEBRATION 1000! Please write to us at the address shown below.

Happy reading!

Anne Canadeo
Senior Editor

Please address questions and book requests to:
Silhouette Reader Service
U.S.: 3010 Walden Ave., P.O. Box 1325, Buffalo, NY 14269
Canadian: P.O. Box 609, Fort Erie, Ont. L2A 5X3

DANIEL'S DADDY
Stella Bagwell

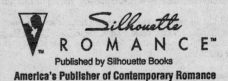

Silhouette
R O M A N C E™
Published by Silhouette Books
America's Publisher of Contemporary Romance

To my son, Jason, with love

SILHOUETTE BOOKS

ISBN 0-373-19020-4

DANIEL'S DADDY

Copyright © 1994 by Stella Bagwell

STELLA BAGWELL

lives with her husband and teenage son in southeastern Oklahoma, where she says the weather is extreme and the people friendly. When she isn't writing romances, she enjoys horse racing and touring the countryside on a motorcycle.

Stella is very proud to know that she can give joy to others through her books. And now, thanks to the Oklahoma Library for the Blind in Oklahoma City, she is able to reach an even bigger audience. The library has transcribed her novels onto cassette tapes so that blind people across the state can also enjoy them.

Fabulous Fathers

Jess Malone On Fatherhood . . .

Daniel,

When you first came into this world, it was just you and me.
A man who didn't know one thing about fatherhood, or even
know what it was like to have a responsible father of his own.

But I told myself I could do it. And somehow we made it
through that first year of diapers, bottles and teething. I began
to think I was actually getting the hang of it. Fatherhood wasn't
going to be all that hard. It was nothing to be afraid of. Then
you started walking and talking, and you grew into this little
person with a mind all your own.

You told me you wanted a mother. And though I hated like hell
to take a wife, I did, because I'd sworn to be the best father to
you that I could be. Because I wanted you to have what I never
had. Parents to love you and always, always be there for you.

You've given me a lot, son—you and your mother. And now
I've learned that being a father is more than showing you how
to hit a baseball or tie your shoes. It's also showing you how
to love.

                                                    Daddy

Chapter One

Hannah Dunbar clutched the neck of her raincoat and shivered against the blast of wet wind swooping down on the graveside mourners. She didn't really know why she'd made a point of coming to the funeral. She'd barely known Frank Malone, even though he'd been her neighbor for so many years. The few times she'd visited with him, he'd been closer to drunk than sober. And although Hannah hated drunkenness, she'd looked beyond the man's vice and come to bid him a final farewell. She guessed it was the least she could do. And then there was Jess. She'd come for him, too. Though she suspected her presence meant little, if nothing at all, to him.

Across the open grave, standing apart from the rest, Jess Malone looked around at the small group of mourners. He was surprised that a dozen or so people had shown up and he wondered why any of them had made the effort. Out of friendship to his father?

Certainly the three men across from him, Bill Barnes, Floyd Jones and Walt Newman, had been old friends. In fact, they were the only friends who'd stayed in contact with Frank after he'd become a recluse.

But the rest of the group? Jess couldn't say. Maybe they were here out of curiosity. Maybe they'd even expected Jess's mother to show up for her ex-husband's burial.

If that was the case, they'd been disappointed, Jess thought cynically. He could have told them that once Betty Malone had walked out on her husband and son, she'd totally wiped them from her existence.

Jess's green eyes slid over the vaguely familiar faces until he reached the end of the group where a tall, slim woman stood apart from the rest. Her flaming red hair had been whipped by the wind. Loose tendrils, which had been torn from the single French braid at the back of her head, curled wildly around her face and shoulders. A drab gray raincoat hid most of her dark dress, while a worn pair of penny loafers covered her feet. The wind was playing with the hem of her dress, exposing a portion of her legs. They were nice legs, he decided, his gaze lingering on their long, sleek curves. Too nice to be hidden by such dowdy clothing.

The murmur of nearby voices jolted him back to the reality of where he was, and he pulled his eyes up to the woman's face.

Hannah Dunbar! If he'd been studying her face as intently as her legs, he would have already recognized the woman who lived across the street from his father. What was *she* doing here?

The question was instantly forgotten as a tug on Jess's hand brought his attention to Daniel, who'd been standing quietly beside him, but was now looking up at him with a lost, bewildered look on his face.

Jess reached down and lifted the small boy into his arms, finding comfort in having his son close to him. The boy would never have a grandfather. Not that Frank could have been one. But now the chance or hope of that ever happening was gone.

"Let us pray."

The minister's request had Jess bowing his head and clutching his son even closer. It was just him and Daniel now.

Draping her coat over the back of a kitchen chair, Hannah crossed the small room and began to fill the coffee machine with water and coffee grounds. After she'd switched it on, she lit a small gas heater in the living room.

It was unusually cool for Lordsburg, New Mexico, even if it was mid-January. Hannah couldn't ever remember feeling this chilled, even counting the time she'd gone to Ruidoso on a trip with the senior class. And that had been more than fifteen years ago.

Jess Malone had been on that trip, too, she recalled, her expression thoughtful as she held her cold hands out to the heater. That year had been his last in Lordsburg. She hadn't seen him since. Until today at the funeral.

He'd changed. That much had been obvious. Fifteen years was a long time. Now that he was thirty-three, he was more muscular and his thick brown hair far shorter than the way he'd worn it as a teenager. His face had changed, too. It was leaner, rougher and more damnably handsome than she remembered. But she'd expected most of those changes in him. What Hannah hadn't expected to see was a child in his arms.

Jess was the last boy in their class that she would have described as a father figure. But obviously the child was his. The minister officiating the memorial service had spoken of the boy as a surviving grandchild to Frank, and since Jess was an only child, that left just one conclusion. So where was the mother, Hannah wondered. She hadn't heard anything about a surviving daughter-in-law. Could Jess be divorced? Widowed?

That's none of your business, Hannah, she hastily scolded herself. A man like Jess would never be her business. She was awkward, shy, just plain old unattractive. If a man did happen to look at her twice, it was for all the wrong reasons. She'd learned that the hard way.

Jess threw his jacket at the end of a grungy plaid couch, then pushed his fingers wearily through his damp hair. He hated this damn house, he thought as he glanced around the small, cluttered room. It reminded him of the isolated, pitiful life his father had led.

Frank had spent most of his time sitting in this dusty old house. Drinking. Grieving over a woman who'd walked out on him and his small son years before. After Jess had grown into a young man, he'd often tried to reach out to his father, to try to help him get past the torment that made him reach for a bottle too often. But Jess had never been able to make his father see what he was doing to himself. He'd continued on a downward spiral, until finally the alcohol had taken him over completely. These past ten years, Frank had rarely been sober.

No woman was worth it, Jess told himself bitterly. There wasn't a woman on this earth who could ever move him to drink himself to addiction, to give up on life.

Sighing, he took a seat on the couch. "Come here, son. Let's get you out of that wet jacket."

"I'm hungry, Daddy," Daniel said as he obediently sidled up to his father.

"I know you are. I'll see what I can find in the kitchen in a few minutes. Why don't you go to the bathroom and wash your hands."

The dark-headed boy looked at his father. "My hands aren't dirty. See?"

He held up his small hands for inspection and Jess shook his head.

"How do you know they aren't dirty?" Jess asked.

Daniel tilted his head to one side as though his father's question didn't make sense at all. "Because you can't see it."

Normally, Jess found his son's logical, nearly four-year-old mind amusing, but today he could hardly force a smile on his face. Even though Jess had been expecting it, the death of his father had shattered him. Not that they were close. It was hard to be close to a man who was more concerned with drowning his sorrows in a bottle than being with his son. Still, he'd loved his father. Alcoholic or not, he was going to miss him terribly.

He looked accusingly at Betty Malone's photo still sitting atop the dusty television. Women were to be enjoyed by man, not cherished. At least Jess knew that, even though his father had never learned it.

"Some kinds of dirt you can't see," Jess said. "So you'd better go wash to make sure."

Daniel frowned but didn't argue the point. Instead, he scampered off toward the bathroom, making zooming noises all the way.

Jess leaned back against the couch and let his gaze drift once again to the picture of his mother. He'd never really known the woman. She'd left him and his father long before Jess was old enough to build memories of her. It would be the same with his own son, he realized with a pang of bitter resentment. Michelle, Daniel's mother, had skipped out on them as soon as she was able to leave the hospital.

It wasn't the way Jess had planned or hoped it to be. Early in their relationship, Michelle had insisted she loved him, and when she'd unexpectedly gotten pregnant, Jess had wanted to marry her. He'd wanted her, himself and the baby to be a family. But Michelle had balked at making such a big commitment. It had been all he could do to talk Michelle out of an abortion.

His mouth twisted with the memory. He'd hoped that Michelle would change as her pregnancy advanced. That her mothering instinct would kick in. It hadn't. She'd resented the nausea, the weight gain, the sheer confinement of her condition. By the time she'd gone through the pain of giving birth, she'd told Jess she was leaving. She didn't want to be a mother. So she'd gone, leaving Jess with a newborn and a hard-learned lesson.

But that had happened almost four years ago. He'd put Michelle and her irresponsibility behind him. Daniel was happy and healthy and Jess was going to make sure that he stayed that way. He was determined to see that the boy didn't grow up feeling as unloved and unwanted as Jess had. No matter that the only family they had was each other.

Rising and entering the kitchen, Jess started to put a sandwich together for Daniel when a knock sounded on the front door. He went to answer it, Daniel following closely on his heels.

"Hello, Jess."

Jess stared at the woman standing on the small slab of concrete outside the door. He'd expected it to be one of his father's old cronies. Not Hannah.

"May I . . . come in?" she asked hesitantly.

Jess noticed a swathe of color flooding her cheeks as she spoke. Apparently, this woman was still as shy as she'd been back in high school. It only made him wonder how she'd summoned enough courage to come over here.

He pushed open the screen door, then stood aside to allow her entry. "It's been a long time. I almost didn't recognize you at the cemetery."

Because he'd been too busy looking at her legs, he thought with self-disgust. What was the matter with him, anyway? Ogling a woman at his father's graveside! What had the worry and strain he'd been through the past few days done to him?

Hannah found it hard to believe that Jess hadn't immediately recognized her. She looked exactly as she had in high school, just a little older. But then, Jess Malone had rarely ever glanced her way. She'd been quiet and awkward then, too. Nothing like the sort that had interested him.

"You do remember that my name is Hannah?"

"Yes. I remember." Even though she'd lived across the street from him and they'd gone to the same school, Hannah Dunbar had never really crossed his mind after he'd left Lordsburg. He almost felt guilty about that, though he couldn't understand why.

He turned back to her and Hannah very nearly gasped. He seemed so big now that she was in the house and standing only a foot away from him. Her heart fluttered as she looked up at his dark face.

"I—noticed that no one—" She swallowed and started again. "I thought you might enjoy some coffee and cake." She thrust a thermos and a foil-wrapped package at him.

Jess's first instinct was to tell her he wasn't the least bit hungry. He wasn't in the mood to visit with anyone. But as his gaze connected with her liquid gray eyes, he stopped himself. She looked like a skittish doe, ready to bolt at his slightest move. Was she afraid of him? Surely not. More than likely she was afraid he would refuse her offer of sympathy.

He took the thermos and package from her and it was then that Hannah noticed the boy standing a few steps away. His forefinger in his mouth, he was carefully studying her. She smiled at him, her love for children automatically brightening her face.

"Hello," she said, holding her hand out to him.

The child immediately came to her. "My name is Daniel Malone," he told Hannah proudly.

She shook Daniel's hand in grown-up fashion, which, by the look on his little round face, obviously impressed him. "It's nice to meet you, Daniel," she said, then looked at Jess.

"Would you like to join us, Hannah? I was just making Daniel a sandwich."

Join them? All sorts of thoughts ran through Hannah's head as her gaze skittered over Jess's face. This morning, she hadn't really planned to do more than attend Frank Malone's funeral. She hadn't thought it prudent to come over to the Malone house and offer her condolences to Jess and his son in person. But as she'd waited for her coffee to brew, she'd looked out the living-room window and noticed that not one car was sitting in the driveway to the old house. The man had just lost his father, and it looked as though no one cared. She didn't like to think of anyone so alone. Not even an outlaw like Jess Malone.

"Well, I suppose I could. Mrs. Rodriguez gave me the rest of the afternoon off. She runs the child day-care center I work for."

Jess motioned his head toward an open doorway just behind them. "The kitchen is through here."

Hannah followed him, glancing tentatively around her as she did. The house was in bad shape. There was no other way to put it. She wondered what Jess thought about the place, then wondered even more how he'd felt about his alcoholic father.

In the kitchen, Daniel climbed upon a chair and scooted eagerly up to the table. Jess set down the thermos and package, then reached to help Hannah off with her raincoat.

She'd never had a man help her with such a personal task. Hannah felt heat flush her face as his hands lightly brushed her shoulders.

"I'm—sorry about your father," she said quietly, not really knowing what to say to this man who'd rarely spoken to her during the years he'd lived in Lordsburg.

At that moment, Jess realized she was the first person who'd said that to him and really meant it. A few of the border patrolmen who worked with him back in Douglas had mouthed the words. But they hadn't known Frank Malone and they'd merely expressed sympathy out of courtesy. He had a feeling Hannah was too reserved to bother saying something she didn't mean.

"I am, too, Hannah." In fact, he was sorry about a lot of things, he thought wearily.

He pulled out a chair for her, and Hannah dropped gracefully into it.

"I have to confess I hadn't seen your father in several months. The last time I tried to visit with him—well, he was—"

"Drunk?" he asked, one dark eyebrow arched mockingly at her embarrassed face.

Nodding, she shifted uncomfortably on the wooden chair. "I was going to say inebriated."

"A different word doesn't make it any less ugly," Jess told her.

Bitterness laced his words, making Hannah feel even more awkward. She'd been crazy to think she could offer a man like Jess Malone any sort of sympathy. He'd been around and she'd been nowhere. What could she say to him that might help or make a difference?

He set a sandwich and a glass of milk in front of Daniel. "There you go, sport," he told the boy. "We'll have a big supper tonight."

"Pizza," Daniel said hopefully.

Jess shook his head. "No. Not pizza. You'd eat that stuff three times a day if I'd let you."

Watching Jess and the child, Hannah once again wondered about Daniel's mother. Where was she? Or had Jess simply adopted a child on his own? She quickly discounted that notion with a mental shake of her head. Daniel resembled Jess very closely. He had the same dark hair and green eyes. Even the dimple in his left cheek was a carbon copy of Jess's.

After setting two thick coffee cups on the small chrome and Formica table, Jess opened the thermos Hannah had given him.

She watched him pour out the hot drink before she ventured to speak. "You know, alcoholism is ugly but you need to remember it's an illness," she said quietly.

"Yeah. An illness," he said, his voice rough with emotion.

Hannah watched him keenly as he took a seat beside Daniel and directly across from her. The pain on his face was at complete odds with the tough-guy image of him she'd always held in her mind.

He pushed one of the cups across the table to her. "The old man should have been strong enough to overcome it," he went on after a minute.

Hannah took a sip of the coffee, then decided she might as well be frank. That was often the best way to help a person. "Perhaps you should have been strong enough to help him."

Jess stared at her. Where did this timid woman get off saying such a thing to him? "Me strong enough! You think I didn't try to get my father off the booze? Let me tell you, Hannah Dunbar, I tried to help him. My father didn't want to be helped!"

She looked at him, her gray eyes full of compassion. "Then you have nothing to feel guilty about."

Jess couldn't believe this woman. How had she known he'd been feeling guilty about his father's death? And how had she found the nerve to tell him so? During high school, he couldn't remember her saying much to anyone, and when she'd spoken to him, he figured that was because they were neighbors. Mostly, she'd been a loner with her nose constantly stuck in a book.

"What did you do after we got out of high school, become a part-time psychologist?"

Hannah's spine stiffened at his mocking question. Maybe she hadn't gone places and maybe she did still live in the same little stucco house she'd shared with her mother. That didn't mean she wanted to be insulted by the likes of him!

"Hardly," she said crisply.

"This was my grandpa's house," Daniel spoke up, interrupting the tension between the two adults. "He was old and sick. But I wish he was here."

Hannah's heart went out to the child who was still too small to understand what losing a loved one was all about.

She longed to move around the table and hold him in her arms.

"Yes, I wish he was here, too," Hannah agreed softly, then offered him a smile. "How old are you, Daniel?"

He held up three fingers. "Daddy says I'll be four soon."

"February," Jess told Hannah with an indulgent grin for his son.

"That old!" Hannah exclaimed, always finding it easy to talk to children. "Why, you'll be in school soon."

"I can say my ABCs already," Daniel told her between gulps of milk. "And I can count, too!"

"Really? You must be a smart little boy," Hannah said.

His head bobbed up and down with childlike conceit. "I am. Wanna hear me count?"

Jess looked at his son with mild surprise. He'd never seen him open up to a stranger like this. Especially a woman. "Not now, Daniel. Eat your sandwich and let Hannah drink her coffee."

Hannah gave Daniel a conspiratorial wink, then reached for the small loaf of pumpkin bread she'd carefully wrapped in aluminum foil. "If you'll fetch me a knife," she told Jess, "I'll slice this for us."

He got up from his seat and rummaged around in a cabinet drawer. With his back presented to her, Hannah took the liberty of looking at him. A white shirt with navy blue pinstripes covered his broad shoulders. It was tucked into a pair of dark trousers and Hannah couldn't help but notice his trim waist and firmly muscled hips.

Jess Malone was certainly good to look at, she decided. But that didn't mean a whole lot to her. Hannah wasn't one to admire men. The one time she had—well, that was an experience Hannah wished with all her might that she could forget.

Jess returned to the table with a small paring knife and offered it to her. Hannah thanked him and quickly sliced off two thick pieces of the sweet, nut-filled bread. When she glanced inquiringly at Daniel, Jess nodded, so she cut a piece for the boy, too.

"You're probably thinking I haven't accomplished much since we graduated high school. I mean—me working in a day-care center."

Jess glanced at her fine-boned hands as she cut the dessert. There was no wedding ring on her finger, which didn't surprise him. He imagined Hannah Dunbar was just as virginal now as she had been fifteen years ago. He would have found that idea amusing back then. Now it both saddened and intrigued him. No person should be *that* alone, he thought.

"I wasn't thinking that at all. In fact, I admire anyone that works with children," he said, his eyes moving from her hands to the thrust of her small bosom, then finally to her face. Hannah Dunbar was far from ugly. In fact, he figured she could be a looker if she'd let her hair loose and throw away that matronly dress she was hiding behind.

That idea had his thoughts going one step further and his gaze made a slow appraisal of her slender figure. What would Hannah look like without that dark print dress that buttoned tightly at her throat?

Jess mentally shook his head, wondering again where these strange thoughts were coming from. What was it about this woman that kept turning his mind to sex?

"Well, I could understand if you had been thinking that about me," she said with a sigh. "I haven't been anywhere but here in Lordsburg since we graduated."

Her gaze connected with his as she handed him a slice of pumpkin bread, and in that moment it dawned on her that she'd never seen such green eyes on a man before. They were moss green, deep and clear, and very disarming.

You don't admire men, she quickly reminded herself, especially their eyes. So why are you looking at Jess's? Hannah couldn't answer that question. She only knew there was something about the bad boy in him that had always intrigued her. She could admit that much to herself, but no one else. She likened the weakness to Eve's fascination for the Serpent.

"Staying in one place isn't a crime," he said, then eased back in his chair. "I don't suppose you ever married?"

Jess took a bite of the bread. As he chewed and waited for her to answer, his eyes slowly studied her face.

She shook her head. "No. I guess I just turned out not to be the marrying sort."

Hannah watched his eyebrows move slightly upward, indicating her words had surprised him.

"You never did like guys very much, did you?" he asked casually.

Did he honestly think that was the reason she hadn't married? Because she didn't like men? Dear Lord, if he only knew how many years she'd dreamed that some good man would ask her to be his wife. But it had never happened and it hurt too much to ever tell him such a thing.

Lifting her chin, she said, "I never liked them as much as you seemed to like women."

To her surprise, he threw back his head and laughed. "Apparently, my old reputation is still alive in Lordsburg."

Color flooded Hannah's cheeks and she quickly looked away. Where was all this stuff coming from? How could she be saying such things to him? Just because she remembered a wild, teenage boy by the name of Jess Malone didn't mean she knew the man across from her.

Clearing her throat, she said, "I don't know why I—I shouldn't have said that." Still unable to look at him, she grabbed her coffee and took a quick gulp.

"So you work at a day-care center. Do you like it?"

She glanced at him, wondering if he was actually curious or if he was merely trying to keep the conversation going. He smiled at her and a funny little feeling unfurled in her midsection.

"Yes, I do. I used to have a job keeping books for a local insurance man. But I like working with children a lot better. And it's something that didn't require I get a college education."

Hannah didn't go on to tell him that children showed her unconditional love and affection, something her lonely heart craved. The last thing she wanted was for Jess Malone to feel sorry for her.

"It surprises me that you didn't leave here to go to college," Jess said. "In school, I remember you always had a book in front of your face and you nearly always made the highest grades."

The fact that he had any memories of her at all warmed Hannah. During those years at school, boys had looked through or around her as though she were invisible. Except for Jess. He'd been the only one who'd taken the time to speak to her now and then. Hannah had never known why. In her teenage heart, she'd wanted to think it was because he'd liked her. But now, after all these years, she figured it was because he was the only boy confident enough in himself to speak to a girl like her. He'd never worried about his reputation. He'd pretty much done and said what he pleased and no one would have dared to suggest he do otherwise.

Oh, yes, Jess had been something back then, she thought. And from what she could see now, he still was.

"I used to think you'd end up like one of those women we had to read about in history class," Jess went on when she didn't say anything. "Like Madame Curie, or somebody like that."

A shy smile curved her lips as she glanced across the table at him. "I was a simple girl. I still am."

Not really wanting to say more, Hannah turned her attention to Daniel, who was nearly finished with his sandwich.

Jess took a drink of his coffee and quietly studied her from the corner of his eye. He doubted the day-care job paid her very much. But then, Hannah probably didn't have many wants beyond the basic necessities. Maybe that explained her lack of motivation to go on to college, Jess thought.

Obviously, Hannah was far from the glamorous, socializing type who wanted to spend money on sexy dresses and lingerie, perfume and weekly visits to the beauty salon. The fact that she was still living in this desert town, in the same run-down stucco house she'd lived in with her mother, told him more about her than she could have told him herself.

"How is your mother doing these days?"

Hannah looked at him, and it dawned on her that he really had lost all contact with this place. "She died a little over a year ago."

Jess didn't know what to say. He hadn't known that Rita Dunbar had died.

"I didn't know," he said quietly.

Looking down at her coffee cup, Hannah shook her head. "No. With your living away, you couldn't have known. Besides, Mother was—"

With a small shake of her head, she broke off, as though speaking of her mother was anything but easy. Jess was surprised at the pang of compassion shooting through him. For years, it had been rumored that Hannah's mother once worked in El Paso as a lady of the evening and as far as Jess knew, Rita had never denied it. He remembered how everyone in Lordsburg had been watching Hannah, expecting her to follow in her mother's illicit footsteps. It was no wonder, he thought, that she'd gone to such extremes to be as unlike Rita as she could be.

"What happened?"

Hannah said, "She died from heart complications."

Jess frowned. "So she'd been ill?"

Hannah looked at him with the realization that he hadn't known about her mother. "She was partially paralyzed. I think being immobilized for so long contributed to her heart disease."

He slowly shook his head. It was hard to imagine Hannah's beautiful, vibrant mother being confined to a wheelchair, or even a pair of crutches.

"What happened?" he asked. "I mean, how did she become disabled?"

Hannah's voice was quiet and matter-of-fact. "She was in a car accident about a year after you left Lordsburg."

That had been fourteen years ago! No wonder Hannah was still in this town, Jess thought. She'd stayed because of her mother.

The information had him looking at her in a totally different light. "My father wasn't one to talk much. He never gave me the news about what was going on around here. I'm sorry I didn't know."

The sincerity on his face touched her. More than she cared to admit. Strange, she thought, how she'd come over here to offer her condolences and had wound up talking about her own loss.

A sad little smile suddenly clouded her features. "So you see," she told him, "I know what you're going through now."

Maybe she did, Jess silently acknowledged. Only her mother hadn't chosen to die like his father, who'd slowly poisoned himself with alcohol.

Hannah pushed back her chair and rose to her feet. "Well, I really must go and I'm sure you have lots of things you need to do."

Jess rose, too, surprised at the faint sense of disappointment running through him. Spinster or not, for a few minutes she'd managed to take his mind off the fact that his father was really gone. He could have talked to her longer. About what, he didn't know. They had nothing in common except they'd both been raised hard in this desert town and both had lost their only parent.

Taking her coat from the back of the chair, Jess helped her into it. As he stood close behind her, he caught a subtle scent of lavender on her hair and skin. It reminded him she was a woman and told him that she wasn't totally without vanity as he'd first imagined.

As soon as Hannah felt his hands leave her shoulders, she stepped away from him and struggled to keep a hot blush from spreading over her face. It shook her to have him so close to her. Men didn't touch her. And to have one like Jess do so, even in a casual way, was very disturbing.

Walking around to Daniel, she passed her fingers gently over the top of his dark head. "I'm glad we met, Daniel. Perhaps before you and your father go home, you can come over and do that counting for me. I have a bird and a cat. You might like to see them, too."

Daniel perked up and looked eagerly at his father. "Can I, Daddy? Can I go see Hannah's house?"

"Maybe. If we have time," Jess told him.

She told Daniel goodbye, then walked out of the kitchen. Jess walked close behind her.

"Thank you for the cake and coffee, Hannah. It was thoughtful of you," he said.

Pausing, she turned to him. "I wanted to do it," she explained simply.

"Not many people—" He stopped, looked away from her, then swallowed as the utter loss of his father swept over him once again. "When my father became a recluse, he lost touch with everybody around here. I'm glad you remembered him."

He looked at her then and Hannah was surprised at the ache of grief she felt for him. "Like I said, I wanted to do it, Jess. And if you . . . need my help for anything, let me know. I go to the cemetery quite often, so I'll keep an eye on your father's grave for you . . . if you'd like."

Once again, he was struck by her genuine kindness. There weren't too many people like her left in the world. People who did things for others simply out of the goodness of their hearts and not for something in return.

"I'd appreciate that very much," he said, feeling more awkward than he could ever remember. He'd never been around a woman like Hannah before and he wasn't quite sure that he'd behaved as he should have. But what the hell, he'd be leaving in a couple of days. He'd more than likely never see Hannah again. Besides, when had it ever mattered to him what a woman thought about his manners? Women were something to be enjoyed, not worried over, he reminded himself.

She reached out her hand. He extended his and she quickly shook it. "Goodbye, Jess," she said, her eyes shyly skittering away from his. "And good luck to you."

"Goodbye, Hannah."

She turned to continue toward the living room. Jess took a step after her. "I'll see you out," he said.

She shook her head. "No. That's not necessary. Enjoy your coffee."

Jess stood and watched her go on out the door. What a strange visit, he thought. And how different Hannah Dunbar was from the vague memories he had of the pale, skinny girl who sat alone in the school cafeteria and ate her lunch out of a brown paper bag. The girl he'd sometimes winked at just to see her blush.

The memory caused a corner of his mouth to curve into a wan smile. Maybe he remembered more about Hannah Dunbar then he realized.

Chapter Two

By nightfall the rain had stopped. Jess took Daniel to a nearby café where home-cooked meals were served smorgasbord-style. Jess was glad to see Daniel hungry and eating his fried chicken and accompanying vegetables. He'd been afraid the trip up here and the ordeal of the funeral might have upset Daniel, but thankfully his son seemed to be taking it all in stride.

They had ice cream for dessert, then Jess, deciding neither he nor Daniel was ready to go back to the old house just yet, drove the two of them out on the interstate for a few miles. The desert highway was more or less empty, other than a freight train headed west. Stopped at the railroad crossing, Daniel watched the long line of cars until it disappeared into the far darkness. After that, Jess turned their truck back toward Lordsburg. He still had a lot of things in his father's house he needed to go through and the sooner he could get it done and over with, the better he'd like it.

"Can we go to Hannah's house now?" Daniel asked, breaking into his father's dismal thoughts.

Surprised by the request, Jess looked at his son. "You must have really liked Hannah," he said.

Daniel nodded. "She was nice."

"You think so, huh. Well, I think she thought you were nice, too."

Daniel bounced his legs up and down on the vinyl seat. "I wish Hannah could be my mommy."

Jess very nearly slammed on the brakes. "You what!"

"I wish she could be my mommy," Daniel repeated with exaggerated patience. "You know I don't have one."

Jess let out a weary breath. Oh, do I ever know it, he thought guiltily. "I know you want a mommy, son. But I—" He stopped midsentence and glanced curiously at Daniel. "Why do you wish Hannah could be your mommy?"

The little boy shrugged one shoulder, then the other. "Just because. Because she's nice. And she smells good. And she's pretty."

So Daniel thought Hannah was pretty and he wanted her to be his mother. Jess couldn't have been more shocked. Not because Daniel had asked outright for a mother. He'd been hounding Jess for some time now on the subject. But he'd never gone so far as to pick out a specific woman for the role. And Hannah was very different from any of the women Daniel had been around, including Louise, the woman who'd been his baby-sitter since the child's infancy. What was it about Hannah that had prompted Daniel to say such things?

"Well...I guess that is true," Jess began slowly, knowing if he didn't say something soon, Daniel would start to question him. "Hannah is nice and pretty." Jess had never thought of her as pretty, but through the eyes of a child, people often looked different. And now that he thought about it, he had to admit that there was something about her that stirred him, too. Something soft and feminine and even sexy. "But I really doubt she wants to be a mommy."

"Why?"

Jess stifled a sigh. He should have been expecting that. "Why? Well, she's not married. And only married ladies want to be mommies."

"Then you could marry her, Daddy. Louise says if you got married, I'd get a mommy."

Jess silently cursed the older woman for opening her mouth about such things to Daniel. And how on earth could a boy who wasn't quite four yet remember such a thing?

"Well, that's true," Jess was forced to agree. "But I don't want to get married."

Daniel folded his little arms across his chest and pushed out his lower lip. Jess braced himself for the whining and pleading to come. But after one, then three, then five miles passed and Daniel remained stubbornly quiet, Jess ventured a hopeful look at his son.

"We're still buddies, aren't we?"

"Yeah," Daniel said, but without much enthusiasm.

"You haven't forgotten that we're going to that baseball game when we get home. Tracie and Dwight will be there."

Jess's friend, Dwight, was also a fellow border patrolman and Tracie was his wife. Since they didn't have any children yet, the couple doted on Daniel. And Daniel was crazy about them. But tonight, the mention of their names only brought a glum nod from Daniel.

After that, Jess decided the best thing to do was let the matter drop. In a few days, when Daniel was back at home with Louise, he'd forget all about this thing with Hannah. Jess couldn't start worrying and fretting just because Daniel *thought* he wanted one certain woman to be his mother.

He wasn't going to worry, Jess muttered to himself as he turned the truck down a residential street. Who was he kidding? He worried about Daniel all the time. He was constantly asking himself if he was doing the right things for his son, spending enough time with him, teaching him what he should know and more than anything, giving him the love he knew the child needed.

A kid needed love from two parents. Jess knew that better than anyone. So he made an extra effort to give his son his time and his affection. But that was hard to do when his job demanded he work long hours. And in two weeks, Louise was moving to Tucson to live with her sister.

Two weeks? No, it was less than two weeks now, he realized. That's how long he had to find some kind, gentle, trustworthy woman to take care of his son. Lord, how was he going to do it? It had been so easy with Louise. She lived right next door to him. She was always home and available to keep Daniel at any hour Jess called upon her. He didn't have to be told that it was going to be nearly impossible to find someone to replace her.

Daniel wants a mother. Yeah, he probably did, Jess answered the voice inside him. Not probably, he *did* want a mother, Jess corrected himself. But Daniel needed to learn he couldn't go around picking a woman to be his mother just because she was nice and smelled good. Besides that, Jess wasn't about to let some woman tie him up in emotional knots again. And he sure as hell wasn't going to let one into Daniel's life, then have her tear his heart apart by leaving. No way. It was better for him not to have a mother at all than to have one who would skip out on them when the going got rough.

A few moments later, Jess pulled into the driveway of his father's house. He and Daniel climbed out of the truck and started walking over to the porch. Lord, the place looked bleak. This was the place Jess had once called home, but now it seemed not much more than a run-down piece of real estate. A big part of the stucco was eroding, leaving shallow pits and holes in the outside walls of the house. The gables hadn't seen paint in years, and the yard, what little there was of it, was nothing more than sand with a few clumps of sage and grama grass growing here and there. Looking the way it did, he knew it was going to be hard to sell the property.

Jess glanced over his shoulder at Hannah's house. A couple of lights were on behind the lace curtains at the windows and Jess wondered what she did in her spare time. What would he find her doing if he went over there right now?

The question left him grunting with amusement. Whatever it was, he'd bet it wasn't entertaining a man.

He unlocked the door, but before he pushed it open, he glanced over at Hannah's once again. Daniel was right in one respect, he thought. Someone like her was just what he needed to take Louise's place. He'd bet his life that Hannah would be dependable. She probably never raised her voice, and judging by the sweet bread she'd brought over today, she could obviously cook, so Daniel wouldn't constantly be fed snack foods. Too bad she lived in Lordsburg instead of Douglas, he thought.

Hannah couldn't sleep and she didn't know why. She'd read for hours, drank herbal tea and watched a boring late-night talk show on TV, but she was still wide-awake.

She blamed her restlessness on Frank Malone's funeral.
She hated funerals. But then, who didn't? However, she'd
especially hated this one because it had reminded her of her
mother's funeral; only a handful of mourners there, no
family except one lonely offspring.

Poor Jess. She hurt for him because she knew how alone
he must be feeling. And poor little Daniel. He would grow
up without his grandfather.

As if the lights across the street were beckoning her,
Hannah walked over to the picture window and looked
out. Jess was still up. Though she couldn't detect him
through the curtainless windows, she could see parts of the
cluttered living room. What was he doing at this hour? It
was after two in the morning.

Was he so upset over his father's passing, he couldn't
rest? Hannah hated to think so. Although his son was with
him, he was more or less alone and she wondered why.
Surely he had someone to whom he was close. Someone
who could have come along with him for emotional sup-
port.

For the umpteenth time, Hannah wondered if Jess was
married. After all, he had a son. True, a man didn't have
to be married to have a son, she quickly reminded herself.
But there had to be a woman somewhere, she rational-
ized. So where was she? Back at home, taking care of other
obligations?

That idea made Hannah snort with disapproval. If that
was the case, Jess Malone didn't have himself much of a
wife or lover. Now if Hannah were married to Jess, she
would have never let him and Daniel come here on their
own to deal with their loved one's death.

Lord have mercy, she was losing it, Hannah thought
with a self-deprecating shake of her head. Imagining her-

self as Jess Malone's wife and Daniel's mother! She'd never be married. Much less to a man like him!

The knock at the door had Hannah bolting straight up out of a dead sleep. Her heart beating wildly in her chest, she glanced around, disoriented, until she finally realized she'd fallen asleep sometime early this morning on the living-room couch.

The knock came again. Louder this time.

Hannah wrapped the white plissé robe more tightly around her and hurried to answer the door. When she opened it and saw that the caller was Jess Malone, she very nearly gasped out loud.

"Jess. Is—uh—is something wrong?" Her eyes darted quickly downward at Daniel, who was clinging to his father's hand and smiling broadly up at her.

Jess stared at Hannah. He hadn't expected to wake her at this hour. It was eight-thirty. He'd figured she was an early riser, even on Saturdays. But it was obvious from her appearance that he'd woken her. She looked different. Very different with her long red hair down and curling wildly around her face and shoulders. Although she was holding the robe tightly together at her throat for modesty's sake, Jess couldn't help but notice the way the white material was stretched against her breasts, outlining their feminine shape. Pure male attraction surged through him, blotting out that part of his brain that was telling him to quit staring.

"Uh—no. We were just—" he thrust the empty thermos bottle at her "—returning your thermos."

"Oh, I'd forgotten," she said, then quickly added, "But there was no need for you to bother."

The early-morning breeze caught at her hair and blew it in her face. One of her hands let go of the robe to push it back, allowing the fabric to fall away and expose the smooth skin of her throat.

Needing no further invitation, Jess's eyes slid downward, hoping the wind would do what his fingers were itching to do. Part the robe even more and expose the creamy swell of her breasts.

She blushed furiously as she noticed Jess looking at her. Suddenly, he felt ridiculous because she'd caught him staring. Dear God, he was in trouble when he started fantasizing about a thirty-three-year-old spinster!

"It's—not a bother," he said while inwardly wishing he could kick himself.

Edging behind the doorjamb as much as she could, Hannah said, "I was just waking up. Have you two had breakfast yet?"

Jess shook his head. "We were headed down to McKay's. Would you like to join us?"

Join them! The last time a man had invited her to go out with him had been years ago. And that invitation had been from a man she should have never trusted. But she had, and in the end she'd regretted it. Since that time, she'd avoided men like the plague. If she suddenly showed up at McKay's with Jess Malone and his son, she'd very likely put the whole town into shock.

"That's very nice of you, Jess. But I—it would take too long to get ready."

It was just as well, he thought. He'd only invited her on a crazy impulse, anyway, thinking it would please Daniel to have her company during breakfast. And him, too. Damn it!

"McKay's isn't fancy," he said, trying again. "Just go throw on some jeans. I'll wait for you."

He was serious, Hannah realized, her heart hammering heavily behind her breast.

"I don't know—if I should," she stammered, a part of her hungering for a chance to act like any normal woman, while the other part was terrified because she didn't know how.

Jess didn't know why he was patiently standing here waiting for her answer when she was acting as though he'd just asked her to go to bed with him instead of to share breakfast with him. What could she be worried about? Daniel would be with them.

"Hellfire, Hannah Dunbar! You act like you've never had a man invite you out to breakfast before. Either you want to go, or you don't. Which is it?"

She *hadn't* been invited out to breakfast before. But she could hardly tell him that. If possible, her creamy white complexion grew even redder at the thought. "I—do."

She pushed the screen door open wide and stood back to allow them entry. "Please come in while I change. I'll hurry."

Jess guessed she would hurry. By the time he and Daniel had stepped inside the house, she was scurrying quickly down the hallway, the white robe flapping against her long, slender legs.

Daniel moved away from his father and looked curiously around the room.

"Don't touch anything," Jess instructed as he, too, glanced around the living room, which was filled with antique furniture dating back to the forties. It was all very womanly, he decided as he took in books, flowers and candles scattered randomly around the room, but it wasn't fussy. In fact, it was much homier than his living room back home in Douglas.

"Wow! There's a bird!"

Jess turned around to see Daniel racing over to a bird cage by the picture window.

"He's pretty! Look how pretty he is, Daddy," Daniel exclaimed as he stood admiring a white cockatoo.

"Don't get too close," Jess warned. "He might want your nose for breakfast."

Giggling loudly, Daniel covered his nose with both hands. "He won't get my nose. I'll keep it covered."

Back in the bedroom, Hannah's hands shook as she fastened the buttons on her dress. It was a pink shirtwaist with elbow-length sleeves. Nothing special. But Hannah didn't own anything special, and as for him telling her to throw on jeans, she'd almost laughed. She didn't own a pair of jeans! Those things were for chic young girls who wanted to show off their sexy bodies. Did he really think she could wear them?

"I was wondering," his voice came to her from the living room, "if you knew some church or charity that I could give my father's things to. I stayed up last night packing them. Now all I need to do is load them into the truck."

"Uh…yes," she called loudly back to him. "I do know a place. The church I attend would welcome anything you have to give. I'll show you where it is after we eat."

She pushed her feet into a pair of white flats, then quickly knotted her hair at the back of her head and secured it with bobby pins. She looked dowdy. But that was nothing new. She'd always been less than pretty and felt it would be foolish of her to ever think she could be. She wasn't like her mother, who'd been young-looking and glamorous right up until the day she'd had the car accident.

Jess, who'd been watching the cockatoo with Daniel, turned when he heard Hannah's footsteps.

She smiled tentatively at him. "I'm ready," she said, hoping he'd put her breathlessness down to hurrying.

She had looked far better in the robe with her hair flying around her shoulders, but Jess could hardly tell her something like that. Especially when Daniel was staring at her as though she were a gift from heaven.

"Good, I hope you're as hungry as we are," he said.

"I'm gonna eat pancakes," Daniel said to Hannah as the three of them traveled the short distance to the café.

She smiled at the boy, finding his dimpled grin as charming as his daddy's. "Oh, that sounds good," she told him. "Are you going to eat yours with blueberries or without?"

Daniel made a face and stuck out his tongue. "Yuk! Not blueberries."

Jess glanced over at Hannah, who was sitting as close as she could possibly get to the passenger door. "I think my cooking has ruined Daniel on blueberry pancakes. They didn't turn out too good."

"They were lumpy and burnt," Daniel reminded him.

Hannah laughed and the warm, tinkling sound washed over Jess and lifted his heavy spirits.

"You don't remember that!" Jess joshed his son.

"Yes, I do," Daniel insisted.

Jess chuckled. "Okay, so you do. Just don't go telling Hannah anything else about my cooking. Okay?"

Daniel giggled and Hannah glanced over at father and son. If Jess did the cooking, maybe there wasn't a woman in their lives, Hannah pondered.

Quit your wondering, Hannah quickly scolded herself. It was none of her business whether Jess had a wife or Daniel had a mother. She was merely an old acquaintance, someone who'd just happened to live across the street from Jess while they were growing up. Just because she was having breakfast with the man didn't mean she was anything special to him.

But it did mean something special to Hannah. It had been so long since anyone, other than the women in her church group, had shown her friendship or invited her places.

Looking out the window beside her, she thought back to how many times as a young teenager, she'd imagined herself riding down the street with Jess Malone. The tough, devilishly handsome bad boy that every girl wanted—even the good girls.

Now, here Hannah was, fifteen years later, doing just what she'd once imagined. But why? And where were all those other willing girls? Why was she here in this truck with him and Daniel, instead?

The café was very full, but Jess managed to find an empty booth in the back. After they ordered, the waitress brought coffee, ice water and orange juice to the table. Jess pulled a drinking straw out of one of the glasses of water and stuck it in a glass of juice before handing it to Daniel.

"Do you like living here, Hannah?" Jess asked as he reached for his coffee.

Hannah, who was stirring cream into her coffee, glanced up at him. "Do I like it?" she repeated blankly, not sure what his question was about. "I suppose—I've never lived anywhere else."

"Did you ever think about leaving?"

As her eyes glided over his handsome face, she decided she'd better not take in too much caffeine until their food arrived. She was as shaky as a leaf in a windstorm and looking at him only made it worse. "Not really. It wasn't possible to leave while mother was alive and needed me."

"But she doesn't figure into the picture anymore."

Shaking her head, she curled her hands around the coffee cup. "No. Mother no longer needs me to care for her. But I like my job here and the woman I work for." Briefly, her eyes met his. "Why do you ask?"

Jess shrugged. Why was he asking? Just because he'd had that one wild notion about her and Daniel didn't mean she'd ever consider such an idea. Or would she?

"Just curious. I live in Douglas, Arizona, now."

"I heard someone say a long time ago that you lived in El Paso," she said.

"I did. But I was transferred a few years ago."

She didn't ask him anything, but Jess could see that she wanted to.

"I work for the U.S. Border Patrol," he said, volunteering the information.

"My daddy wears a gun and badge," Daniel told her proudly. "But he won't let me touch the gun 'cause guns are too dangerous."

That jolted Hannah. The last thing she'd expected Jess Malone to be was a lawman. Although Hannah should have known he wasn't the type to sit behind a desk. No doubt a gun and uniform looked perfect on him. And the adventure of it all surely suited him. He seemed like a man who would always need excitement in his life.

"I didn't know," Hannah said to Jess. "Do you like it?"

He nodded, then frowned. "I'd like it if I didn't have to worry about—" He stopped, then glanced at Daniel. Since the boy seemed to have his attention on another table where a couple of young children were breakfasting with their parents, Jess went on. "Leaving Daniel alone."

Something clutched Hannah's heart. "You...mean... like if you had a bad accident?"

Jess grimaced. "I guess that's a nice way of putting it."

"Your job is that dangerous?" she asked, not liking to think that he could possibly get hurt or even killed in the line of duty.

Shrugging, Jess lifted the coffee cup to his lips. "Sometimes. But I'm trained to handle myself, and I doubt my job puts me in any more danger than your average truck driver. Still, there are no guarantees in life and if something should happen to me—well, Daniel would be alone."

Hannah let out a long breath. He was implying that Daniel didn't have a mother! Could that be true?

Jess sipped his coffee, then lowered the cup to its saucer before he continued. He didn't know why he was getting into all of this with Hannah. She was little more than a stranger. Yet something about her gentle face and shy smile encouraged him to confide in her.

"But I've got a more immediate problem," he went on when she didn't say anything. "Daniel's baby-sitter is leaving in a week and a half. She's an older lady and she's decided to spend her retirement with her sister in Tucson. I can't blame her for that. But I don't know what I'm going to do without her. She's helped me with Daniel from the time I first brought him home from the hospital."

Confused and more curious now than ever, Hannah couldn't stop herself from blurting out, "But what about Daniel's mother? Does she have a job, too?"

The question brought a cynical snort from Jess. "I wouldn't know. I haven't seen her in nearly four years."

Hannah gasped before she could stop it. "You haven't? But why?"

He'd often told himself he was over Michelle's desertion. But he hated to admit to anyone, much less another woman, that he and Daniel hadn't been worth a backward glance to Michelle.

"She moved on."

Hannah couldn't have been more shocked. Even if a woman couldn't get along with her husband, did that justify her leaving her newborn son? Hannah couldn't imagine such a thing.

"Oh. I—I'm sorry." Embarrassed by the whole thing, she took a quick, nervous gulp of coffee.

Jess shrugged. "There's no need for you to be sorry, Hannah. We were never married. Michelle didn't want that. She didn't want to be tied down in any way."

Hannah wanted to ask him why he'd involved himself with that sort of self-centered woman, but she stopped herself. She didn't want to sound preachy. Besides, in Hannah's eyes, he'd more than made up for the mistake by being a caring father to Daniel.

"Some people just can't handle responsibility," she said softly. "They don't set out to intentionally hurt others. But they do."

Jess was surprised by her words and her open-mindedness about the whole thing. But then, a lot about Hannah had surprised him.

Before anything else could be said, the waitress arrived with their breakfast. As they ate, Daniel became very talkative and Hannah took pains to answer his many questions. He was a bright, inquisitive boy for his age, and from his conversation, she could tell that Jess had obviously spent a great deal of time with him. That and just the fact that Jess had taken on the job of a single father surprised Hannah greatly. Remembering the teenage Jess Malone, she would have never figured him to be so responsible; he'd grown up. Oh, had he ever.

After the meal was over and the three of them were walking across the parking lot to Jess's pickup, he said, "I feel like I've just come out from under a microscope. I think everyone in that place was looking when we walked out of there. You'd think I was a creature from Mars, or something.''

Hannah felt herself blushing. ''I don't think they were—uh, looking at you, Jess.''

He opened the pickup door. As Daniel climbed in, he glanced at Hannah. ''What makes you say that?''

''Because I know they were looking at me.''

''You? You're not a stranger around here. Probably everyone in that café knew you.''

Hannah felt the familiar hurt and embarrassment rise in her. ''They did know me. That's . . . uh . . . why they were looking. They've never seen me out with a man. I guess they were wondering what I was doing with you.'' Or more likely, what Jess was doing inviting a woman like her out to breakfast, she silently added.

How utterly cruel, Jess thought. ''It's none of their damn business,'' he said with a grimace.

She smiled wanly. ''No. But I've had years to get used to being labeled the weird old maid.''

Hannah Dunbar was far from old and there wasn't anything weird about her that he could see. Certainly reserved and shy, but not weird.

Deciding the best thing to do was treat the situation lightly, Jess gave her an impish wink. ''Maybe they'll think we spent the night together. That'll cut your reputation to shreds.''

Of course he was teasing. Still, just the thought of being *that* intimate with Jess was enough to shake her. ''I really think it would be your reputation that would suffer,'' she tried to joke.

Not wanting her to feel any more awkward than she already did, Jess merely smiled and took her elbow to help her up into the seat. Her arm was small and soft and made him feel oddly protective. This woman was too vulnerable, he thought. And far too kind for her own good.

"Thank you for breakfast," Hannah said when he pulled into her driveway. "It was very nice of you and Daniel to invite me."

"Can I go in with Hannah?" Daniel quickly asked his father. "Can I go see the bird again?"

"*May* I go in," Jess corrected him, then shook his head. "No. You may not go in. You've already talked Hannah's leg off this morning."

"Nonsense," Hannah said as Daniel looked beseechingly up at her. "I won't be doing anything but a little housecleaning. Let Daniel stay with me while you take your father's things to the church."

"You didn't show me where it was," Jess reminded her. "And I forgot to ask."

"Oh. It's the Catholic church on the south end of town. You probably remember it."

Not from attending services, he thought, but rather from circling the old building on his motorcycle. Maybe things would have turned out differently for him if he'd been inside with Hannah, rather than outside giving Judy Mae Johnson a fast ride. Maybe he wouldn't be a single father now. Or maybe Hannah wouldn't be so virginal. That thought brought a curve to his lips and a dimple in his cheek.

"Yeah, I remember. What do I do with the things, once I get there?"

Hannah frowned as she tried to figure out what was putting such a devilish look on his face. They'd been talking about church, for Pete's sake! But this was Jess Malone, she quickly reminded herself. The same guy who'd been accused of seducing his high-school English teacher.

Realizing she had yet to answer his question, Hannah said, "Just set them inside the front door. It's never locked. Father Lopez or one of the other parishioners will find them."

"What about me, Daddy?" Daniel said, tugging on Jess's shirtsleeve. "Do I get to stay at Hannah's?"

"Of course you can," Hannah told the boy before Jess had a chance to protest. "Come on and we'll feed Albert."

"You're sure about this?" Jess asked her while unbuckling Daniel's seat belt. "I wouldn't want either of us to be imposing on you."

Hannah held her arms up to Daniel. The boy scrambled across the seat and straight to Hannah. She helped him down to the ground, then held on to his hand while glancing over to Jess.

"I'm happy for Daniel to visit. And don't worry. I might not be a mother, but I do know how to take care of children."

Jess wasn't worried about that. He was more concerned about Daniel's hanging his sights on having Hannah for a mother.

"I'm not worried," he assured her, then started the truck and backed onto the street.

As he pulled away from the curb, he watched Hannah and Daniel walking hand in hand onto the porch. By the time they reached the door, Hannah was laughing and Daniel was grinning. So much for not worrying, Jess groaned to himself.

Chapter Three

For the next hour, Daniel talked nonstop. But Hannah was used to a child's chatter. Indeed, she was far more comfortable communicating with children than adults—children appreciated her companionship. They didn't expect her to look a certain way and they didn't judge her because she wasn't exactly like their mothers or sisters or aunts.

"I have a tricycle at home," Daniel said as he followed Hannah around the huge old kitchen. "Daddy says it won't be long 'til I can have a bicycle."

"Then you'll be riding on two wheels instead of three," Hannah said as she wiped the front of the refrigerator with a damp sponge.

"Why are you doing that?"

"To make it clean," Hannah explained.

Daniel shook his head. "You're just like my daddy. He makes me wash my hands even when you can't see dirt."

Hannah smiled to herself. "And do you always do what your daddy tells you to do?"

Daniel's chin bobbed up and down. "Yes. 'Cause I'm a good boy."

Hannah squatted on her heels to wash the lower part of the appliance. "I'm sure that you are," she agreed.

"Your hair looks like an apple."

She'd been called carrot top before, but never an apple. "That's because it's red. Do you know what yours looks like?"

She glanced from her work to see Daniel's hands plop on the top of his head.

"No. What does it look like?" he asked, his little face all grins.

"A piece of chocolate."

He giggled loudly over that, then marched over to the kitchen table and sat down. At that moment, Hannah felt a terrible pang of regret. A child had never been in this house. Not much of anybody had been in this house. She hadn't really wanted it that way. For a while after her mother's accident, she thought, even hoped, that some man, a nice, kind man who would appreciate her, would come into her life, give her love and children. It had never happened. Now, after all these years, she knew it never would.

"Are you still hungry?" she asked him, while telling herself she was wrong in feeling a little bit sorry for herself.

"Nope. My daddy will be back soon and then I'll have to leave."

"Then maybe we should go outside and find Oscar before you have to go," Hannah suggested.

Daniel eagerly agreed and followed Hannah out a door leading to the backyard. They found the gray tabby curled up on a ledge of brick surrounding a flower bed. While Daniel made friends with the cat, Hannah sat on the wooden steps and enjoyed the warmth of the bright sunshine.

Nearly a half hour later, Daniel was still playing with Oscar when Hannah heard a vehicle stop in the driveway. By the time she'd herded Daniel and the cat around to the front, Jess had already climbed from the truck and was walking to the porch. When he spotted the three of them, he stopped and gave them all a grin.

"Hey, what's that blob of gray fur you're carrying there?" he asked his son.

Daniel raced to his father. "He's my new friend. His name is Oscar," Daniel told him.

"He looks like a mighty fine friend," Jess said, scratching the lazy tom between the ears.

After a moment, Jess glanced over at Hannah who was standing a few steps away. The desert wind was tugging at her hair, loosening the curly wisps around her face. She met his gaze briefly before looking away and wiping the wayward hair back from her cheeks.

In that moment, it dawned on Jess how everything about her was feminine. From her pink dress and lightly freckled skin to the unruly curls tickling the back of her neck. She was a pretty woman. Why had it taken Daniel to make him see that?

"Sorry I was gone so long. I went by the real estate agency to see about putting the place on the market."

So that meant he planned to get rid of all ties here in Lordsburg. For some reason, the thought made her feel very empty.

"No problem," she said. "Daniel and I have been having a fine time. Haven't we, Daniel?"

"Yeah!" Daniel shouted happily. "See, Daddy, I told you she'd be a good mommy for me."

Jess groaned. Hannah stared at the two of them.

"Uh...Daniel, I want you to play on the porch with Oscar while Hannah and I have a talk," Jess told him, then looked at Hannah who was still wearing a bemused expression. "Is that all right with you?"

Nodding, she turned toward the house. "Why don't we go in and I'll make coffee."

Once in the kitchen, Hannah went straight to work putting the grounds and water together, then setting out cups and saucers.

Ignoring the table and chairs, Jess went over to the back door, folded his arms across his chest and looked out the window.

After a few awkward moments, Hannah said, "You don't have to explain or apologize for anything. I understand that children say the first thing that pops into their heads."

Even though she had her back to him, Hannah could feel his gaze on her. Just knowing he was looking at her sent heat rushing from the roots of her hair all the way down to her toes.

"Actually, I wasn't going to apologize. Since you work with children, I'm sure you know that Daniel is too young to know what—well, you know what I'm trying to say."

Even though her heart continued to race in her throat, Hannah turned to him and nodded that she did understand. But if all this wasn't about an apology, what was it about? And why did he look so—anguished?

"I—" One of his arms lifted and fell as he struggled for a way to begin. "This morning when I asked you whether you liked living here—I did that for a reason."

"Oh?"

"Yes. Well, we got to talking about other things and I decided not to bring it up. But now that Daniel—"

He stopped abruptly and walked over to where she was standing by the kitchen cabinets. Hannah found his closeness so disturbing, she very nearly forgot to breathe. She could smell the musky, erotic scent of his cologne, see the pores in his skin and a faint scar at the bottom of his chin.

Reaching behind her, she grabbed on to the edge of the cabinet to steady herself. "Is there...something you want to ask me?" She desperately wanted him to say what he had to say and leave. Otherwise, she was going to die from lack of oxygen.

"Yes. There is. I'd like to make you a proposition."

Hannah stared at him, her gray eyes wide, her mouth parted. "A proposition? What—what kind?"

Behind him on the cabinet counter, the coffee machine gave its last dying gurgle. Jess's head motioned toward it. "Why don't you get the coffee first," he suggested, "and I'll go check on Daniel to make sure he's staying put."

While Jess was gone, Hannah poured coffee into both cups; however, her hands were shaking so badly, she sloshed the hot liquid onto one of the saucers and part of the tablecloth. In a nervous rush, she grabbed another saucer and sopped at the tablecloth with a dish towel.

She wasn't used to any of this. Especially having a good-looking man in her house. Much less having one make her a proposition of some sort! What could possibly be on his mind? What could all this about Daniel and her willingness to leave Lordsburg be leading up to? Surely he wasn't going to ask her to move to Douglas, her mind raced on. It was too much to imagine!

When Jess returned to the kitchen, he said, "Daniel's fine. But I'm not so sure Oscar will ever be the same."

"Oscar loves anyone who will give him attention. Um...do you take cream or sugar?"

Jess shook his head as he pulled out a chair and sat down. "Black for me," he said, then glanced up at Hannah who was hovering over by the kitchen sink. "Aren't you going to sit down?"

She didn't want to. But it would appear rude if she refused, so she took a seat directly across from him and tried to appear casual as she stirred a spoonful of sugar into her coffee.

"I guess there's no simple way to put any of this," Jess said after a moment. "Other than to come right out and ask..."

He hesitated once again and Hannah's gray eyes lifted to meet his warm green ones. As their gazes locked, her heart gave a sickening jolt.

"Yes?" she urged.

Jess let out a long breath. What the hell was the matter with him, Jess wondered. His job required him to deal with all sorts of people. Men and women. Why was talking to Hannah so difficult? Why did little things about her keep distracting him? Like the way the end of her nose tilted upward, the little brown mole at the side of her mouth.

And that mouth. Why did his eyes behave as if that were the only thing in the room to look at? Hell, he wasn't desperate for a woman. In fact, he didn't want a woman. Certainly not in an emotional way. And physically? Well, who could be less tempting than virginal Hannah?

"I was wondering if you'd be willing to relocate to Douglas?" he finally said.

Hannah suddenly had the sensation that the room was tilting or that she was in a dream. "Relocate? Me move to Douglas?" she asked in a small, shocked voice. "Why would I want to do that?"

Yeah, why would she, Jess asked himself. What gave him the idea that this woman might be willing to do something like that for him? "I thought you might do it for Daniel."

She leaned forward, her eyes wide. "Pardon me?"

Slumping back in his chair, Jess shoved his fingers through his dark, wavy hair. "I thought you might consider taking on the job of being Daniel's—baby-sitter."

The air whooshed from Hannah's lungs. "Daniel's baby-sitter," she whispered, her mind spinning like a tornado.

"I know this has come at you like a bolt out of the blue. But like I said, I'm going to need someone to take Louise's place in a matter of days. And Daniel has taken a real liking to you."

"I like Daniel very much, too. But—" She looked at him, and realized there was a part of her that wanted to say yes, she'd go. But she couldn't listen to that part. She had to listen to the sensible side, the side of her that said she'd been hurt by a man once before because she'd impulsively given in to him. It would be crazy of her to repeat that mistake. "This is my home. It's—the only place I've ever lived."

"I realize that. But you don't have any other ties here, do you? Like someone special?"

If only he were asking her to leave Lordsburg for different reasons, Hannah thought, then gave herself a mental shake for it. She had to get a grip on herself. She had to quit this ridiculous romanticizing about Jess Malone.

"No. There's no one," she admitted. "But I couldn't just leave this house. And I wouldn't know a soul in Douglas."

"You'd know me. And Daniel."

She shook her head as all sorts of doubts and possibilities rushed through her mind. "I'd have to look for housing and it's not easy to find."

"Louise is putting her house up for sale," Jess said quickly.

Hannah looked at him incredulously. Did he think she had money of that sort, or even quick means of acquiring it? "I couldn't buy a house, Jess! At least not until I sold this one, and that might take months or even a year or two."

She was probably right about that, Jess thought. He doubted there was much turnover of real estate in this area. "You could always rent," he suggested.

"Renting is expensive. Besides, I'm not one to make changes." And moving to Douglas would be more than a change, she realized. It would be making a commitment to him and Daniel. And she wasn't sure that would be a wise move.

"Maybe you're not one to make moves or changes," he conceded, "but I sure can't see what's so special about this place."

"It's my home," she said, hoping that would be enough explanation to satisfy him.

"You can make your home in Douglas," he countered.

Who with? Hannah wondered, her gaze dropping to the coffee she'd made no effort to drink yet. But then, who did she really have here in Lordsburg other than the few women friends she worked with?

Hannah didn't say anything and Jess drummed his fingers on the tabletop. He didn't know why this had become so important to him. Maybe because he felt so guilty about Daniel's not having a mother, or maybe it was that hopeful, pleading look that had been in his son's eyes when he'd talked about Hannah. Jess didn't know. He only knew that if Hannah would agree, his son would be happy and well cared for. And Daniel was all that mattered to him.

Before he could change his mind, he said, "Look, if it will help, you won't have to worry about housing. You can live with me and Daniel. Our house has three bedrooms. As far as that goes, it would probably make things easier for all of us if you did, seeing I'm sometimes called out at odd hours of the night."

Live with him and Daniel! The mere thought made her insides shake. Jumping up from the table, she went over to the sink and thrust her hands into the soapy water she'd been using earlier. There was only a bowl, a fork and spoon to be cleaned. Hannah washed each of them twice before she realized she hadn't said a word to him.

"Hannah? What do you think?"

She thought he'd lost his mind, or she'd lost hers. That was it! She'd lived alone for so long, she was starting to hallucinate.

"I—that—" She shook her head, then started again. "I could never do that." She most definitely couldn't do that. He was already making her feel strange. If she was around him every day, there was no telling what would happen. She'd turn into a lovesick calf and make a complete idiot of herself. No way could she ever chance humiliating herself like that. No matter how much she'd enjoy taking care of Daniel.

"Why?"

Something in that one word made her glance over her shoulder at him. Dear Lord, he was good to look at, but at the moment it was the desperation on his face that really got to her. If only he'd been cocky or indifferent, then she would have had little trouble resisting him. But this! He was looking at her as if he really needed her. No man had ever needed Hannah before, and to think Jess did, left an odd new feeling rushing through her.

"It wouldn't be right," she said in a low voice.

Frowning, uncertain that she'd spoken at all, he asked, "Did you say something?"

Hannah drew in a deep breath and turned around to face him. "I said, it wouldn't be right. To live with you."

Jess got up from the table and walked over to her. "My word, Hannah, I'm not proposing anything indecent or immoral here. I just want you to be Daniel's baby-sitter."

Bright red color splotched Hannah's face and throat. No, a man like Jess would never want anything indecent from her. "I—know that. But other people—your friends and neighbors will talk. I'm not so sure it would be good for Daniel."

"Daniel's too young to be affected by gossip. As for me, I say to hell with anyone who talks about other people."

Hannah bit her lip as she thought he was at least partly right. "Maybe. But having a woman in the house might be confusing to Daniel. Especially since—he's never had a mother."

Groaning, Jess lifted his eyes to the ceiling. "If that's the case, then how the hell will he ever *not* be confused?"

"I'm only thinking of Daniel," she reasoned. Although that wasn't quite true. She was also thinking of her own peace of mind. Something told her that if she took on this job, she'd be in danger of losing her heart to Jess and Daniel. It was a terrifying thought.

"Yeah. I guess you are. But right now, I'm more worried about who's going to be there to take care of him when I'm at work, or God forbid, if something should happen to me."

"I understand that. But I'm not the person you need." She swallowed, then bravely lifted her eyes to his. "Forgive me, Jess, if I sound forward, but what you really need is a wife. And Daniel needs a mother.''

Not her, too, he thought with disgust. Didn't he hear that enough from Dwight and Tracie? What did marriage have to do with it, anyway? A woman could see to Daniel's needs without Jess's having to sign a marriage license!

He jammed his hands into the back pockets of his jeans. ''Well, that's not going to happen,'' he said gruffly. ''I'm not about to hook myself up to some woman who may or may not be good for Daniel, just to make things legal. No. That's not for me.''

Hannah could see that her suggestion had raised his hackles. Yet she couldn't help it. She'd only said what she'd truly felt.

''I'm sorry. I guess I spoke out of turn. Your private life is none of my business.''

Jess wiped a weary hand over his face, then gazed at her. She looked edgy and regretful and, oddly enough, almost beautiful as her fingers toyed nervously with one of the buttons on her pink dress.

''No. I'm sorry,'' he said resignedly. ''I should have never laid all this on you. None of this is your problem. Daniel is—''

''Hannah, I think Oscar is hungry. Can we feed him?''

Both adults turned their heads to see Daniel entering the kitchen with the gray tabby trotting close on his heels.

''Daniel, what are you doing bringing that cat into the house?'' Jess demanded, frustration making his voice sharper than he'd intended. ''Hannah might not allow that!''

Daniel shot Hannah an anxious look, which prompted her to go to him, kneel down and kiss his cheek. ''Don't worry,'' she said, smiling and ruffling his hair. ''Of course

I allow Oscar to come in. Bring him over here and I'll let you feed him.''

All smiles, Daniel and Oscar followed Hannah over to the pantry where she got down a plastic bowl and a box of dry cat food.

Bemused, Jess watched his son as Hannah patiently showed him how to feed the cat. It was uncanny how well Daniel and Hannah went together. Much more so than Louise, who took ample care of his son, but had never really been much more than a baby-sitter to him. Jess had a feeling that Hannah would not only see to Daniel's physical needs, she would also fill that emotional part of his life that only a mother could fill. But what good was knowing that when she refused to consider the job?

Damn it, why did women have to be so contrary? And why did men have to need them so?

"You'd better tell Oscar goodbye, son," he said, walking over to the three of them. "We have to get ready to go back home."

Disappointment made Daniel's bottom lip droop and his little shoulders slump. Jess expected his son to start begging to let him stay. However, Daniel surprised him by turning a hopeful look on Hannah.

"When we go home, will you come see us, Hannah? Will you bring Oscar, too? I have a dog. He could play with him and you could play with me."

Hannah felt as if two hands were on her heart, wringing out its last drop of blood. Tears stung her eyes as she looked at the little boy who had somehow managed to endear himself to her in a matter of only a few short hours.

"I don't know, Daniel. Douglas is a long way from here. But—I might drive down there sometime."

From the happy, excited look on his face, Jess knew Daniel had taken her "might" for a yes. He only hoped that once they got back home and into their everyday routine, Daniel would forget all about Hannah. Otherwise, the little boy was going to be very disappointed when she never showed up.

"Yea! Daddy, did you hear? Hannah might come!"

Jess's eyes turned to Hannah and she knew she looked guilty, though she didn't know why. She hadn't out-and-out lied. She might drive down to Douglas. Someday.

"Yeah, I heard, son. C'mon now, so Hannah can get back to her housework." He put his hand against Daniel's back and guided him out of the kitchen.

Hannah followed them to the front door. "I'm glad I got to see you again, Jess. Although I wish it had been under happier circumstances," she said.

"Yes, I do, too," he replied, though he knew, and she did, too, that their paths had crossed only because of his father's funeral. Nor would they ever likely cross again. Strange how he hated to think this would be the last time he'd see her.

Hannah took Daniel's hand and shook it with great importance. "I'm glad I got to meet you, Daniel. You're a fine boy."

Daniel squirmed and wrinkled his nose, then grinned at her. "Daddy says that, too."

Hannah smiled back, and though she wanted to pull him into her arms and give him a fierce hug, she didn't. She feared it might upset him if she got emotional now.

"And your daddy is right."

"Goodbye, Hannah," Jess said.

She looked up at Jess and wondered why those two words felt like a door slamming in her face.

"Goodbye," she said, hoping the ache in her throat didn't sound in her voice.

Father and son turned and went down the steps. Hannah closed the door and watched from the window as they got into the truck and drove across the street. Not until they'd gone into the house and shut the door, did she allow the curtain to fall back into place and block the Malone house from her sight.

They were gone. The house was quiet again, except for Albert who was hopping agitatedly from one side of his cage to the other.

"It won't do you any good to carry on, Albert. We're not going to move to Arizona. We don't have any business there. *I* don't have any business getting involved with Jess Malone. No matter how adorable his son is. Jess Malone is, or at least he was, a playboy. And that's bad news, Albert."

The white bird looked at her, cocked his head to one side, then blinked his eyes. "Bad news!" he squawked loudly.

Hannah jumped to her feet and rushed over to the cage. "Albert! You talked! You rascal, I've been trying to get you to say hello for six months. Now all of a sudden, you come out with two words!"

Instinctively, her eyes were drawn to the house beyond her picture window. It was an omen, she thought. Albert had spoken to warn her. Bad news! She'd been right in turning down Jess's offer. She'd saved herself a big heartache. So why did she have the urge to cry her eyes out?

Jess moved restlessly from one dingy room to the other. He still wasn't sure what to do about his father's furniture and the few things that were left in the kitchen, but since the house would more than likely be on the market for several months, before it sold, he'd have plenty of time to decide.

Maybe he should offer some of it to Hannah, he mused, wiping a hand over a carved-oak buffet dresser. It was a nice piece of furniture, and it was obvious from what Jess had seen of Hannah's place that she loved antiques.

No. Just stop your thinking, Jess, he scolded himself. He wasn't going to call Hannah about furniture or anything else. They'd already told her goodbye and he didn't want Daniel to see her again. The boy had talked about her all evening until Jess had finally put him to bed and read him to sleep.

With a heavy sigh, Jess went into the small living room to give it one last inspection. He'd managed to get rid of all the clutter. Now all that was left was the furniture: a couch, armchair, black-and-white TV, footstool and a scarred coffee table. And that damn picture of Betty. What was he going to do with it?

His father had never moved the thing. As though it were some sort of shrine, or something. As far as Jess was concerned, it was like keeping the rattlers from a snake that had bitten him.

He ought to burn it, Jess thought, lifting the photo and looking at the young, blond woman smiling back at him. There was no doubt that his mother had been beautiful. It was obvious from this picture. But superficial beauty was all she'd been blessed with. She'd certainly not possessed an ounce of compassion or sense of responsibility. From what little his father had told him about her, he knew Betty had worked as a waitress in a local truck-stop café. The first good-looking, fast-talking trucker to come by and offer her a trip to Las Vegas was all it had taken to make her forget about Jess and his father. Apparently, Betty had been all too ready to leave them and this one-horse town behind for bright lights and excitement.

The bitter thoughts drew his eyes toward the window and Hannah's house across the street. Was she *that* different? Well, hell, yes, Jess, she's a *lot* different, he impatiently answered himself. She didn't like men. At least not in the way Michelle had. She wasn't absorbed with herself or her looks. She was a woman with small wants.

That was exactly the kind of woman he needed. No, Jess quickly corrected his assumption. He didn't need her. Daniel did.

What you need, Jess, is a wife. Daniel needs a mother.

Hannah's words spun around in his head like a stuck wheel that couldn't go backward or move forward. It was just there in his mind, bugging the hell out of him.

What did Hannah know about it, anyway? he muttered as he switched on the old television set. She didn't even date, much less know about love and marriage and children.

When the TV screen finally lit up, Jess had settled himself on the couch. The fuzzy picture was an old episode of "Bonanza." Now, there was a man who raised four boys without the help of a woman, Jess thought, as he watched Ben break up a fight between Hoss and Little Joe. If Ben Cartwright could do it, so could Jess Malone.

But that was fiction. It didn't work that way in real life.

Jess's musings were suddenly interrupted by a faint sound from the bedroom. He went quickly to where he'd left Daniel asleep in the narrow twin bed, and switched on a nearby table lamp.

The boy was still asleep, although he was moving restlessly upon the mattress. Jess gently patted Daniel's back until he was settled and quiet, then pulled the tangled covers back up to the child's chin.

Before turning out the light, his gaze was drawn back to his son's sleeping face. He looked angelic. All children looked that way while they were sleeping, Jess thought. Yet this was *his* child. And he loved him fiercely. He would do anything for him. Anything to see that he was healthy and happy.

Anything? Even get married and give him a mother?

Jess switched off the lamp and told himself not to feel guilty. But the truth was he was always feeling guilty about Daniel, and no matter how he tried to look at things realistically, he always came away feeling as though he'd somehow let his son down.

His jaw clenched with determination, Jess went back to the living room and picked up the phone directory. Hannah's number was listed. Before he could ask himself what he was doing or why, he lifted the receiver and dialed the number on the old rotary phone.

"Hello?"

Suddenly, his tongue felt glued to the roof of his mouth, forcing him to swallow before he spoke. "Hannah, it's Jess."

"Jess? Um—what are you doing? Isn't it late?"

Her voice was husky, as though she'd been asleep. Jess glanced at his watch and was shocked to see that it was almost midnight.

"I—didn't realize it was this late. I'm sorry I woke you."

"That's all right." Pushing her tumbled hair out of her face, she raised herself on one elbow. "Is there something I can do for you? Something you wanted to tell me before you leave tomorrow?"

She could do much for him. So very much. Just admitting it to himself lifted a weight from Jess's broad shoulders.

"Actually, there is," he said, deciding there wasn't time for beating around the bush. "Can you come over here?"

Wide-awake now, Hannah sat straight up in bed. "Now? At this hour?"

"Right now."

Her hand went to her tangled hair and she glanced down at her flimsy white nightgown. Did he expect her to just jump out of bed and cross the street?

"Jess, is something wrong with Daniel?"

"No. Except that he wants you to be his mother."

Daniel wanted her for a mother. The very thought of it made Hannah want to cry and smile at the same time.

"I feel very honored that he does. But you and I both know that it's impossible for me to be his mother."

"Why is that?"

He glanced at the TV screen. "Bonanza" was on its final scene. The brothers had settled their differences and father Ben was looking on with a wise, contented smile. He'd done the right things for his boys. Now he could be happy about it.

"Because I didn't give birth to him."

"It takes more than giving birth to be a mother," he said gruffly, then sighed and added in a gentler tone, "And you could be Daniel's stepmother."

It took a moment for his words to sink in. When they did, Hannah began to tremble all over.

"What—what are you saying?"

Shoving his hand through his hair, Jess glanced out the window at her house. Was she still in bed?

"I'm saying that—" He took a deep breath. "I'm telling you that I want you to marry me. Will you?"

Stunned beyond words, Hannah gripped the receiver and glanced wildly around her dark bedroom. "M-marry you?"

"That's right. So what do you say?"

Hannah pressed her hand to her heart. At the rate it was beating, she figured it was either going to jump out of her chest or stop completely. "I'll be right over," she finally managed to say.

The phone clicked in his ear. A thoughtful frown on his face, Jess dropped the receiver onto its hook. She'd be right over. What did that mean? Yes? No?

Jess sat down on the couch to wait.

Chapter Four

Hannah shivered violently as she raised her hand to knock on Jess's door. The night was cold and the gown and robe she wore beneath her raincoat were thin, but Hannah suspected it wasn't the weather that was giving her the shakes—it was the man inside the house.

Hearing her footsteps, Jess didn't wait for her knock, he jumped from the couch and jerked open the door. Hannah stood on the other side of the threshold, staring at him, stunned motionless at the idea that this man silhouetted against the door frame could possibly become her husband.

Before she could utter a word, Jess reached for her arm and yanked her into the house.

"I didn't think you'd ever get over here," he said, shutting the door behind them.

Hannah quickly moved away from him to the middle of the room where she hugged her arms against her waist in an attempt to still her shivers.

"I was in bed," she explained, her expression saying she found his impatience as unbelievable as his proposal.

Yes, Jess could see that she'd been in bed. Her long red hair fell against her back and shoulders in thick, curly waves. Beneath the hem of her coat, the same white robe he'd found her in this morning, brushed against her bare legs.

Breathing deeply, he lifted his gaze to her face.

"Well, you're here now. So what's your answer?"

Hannah's mouth fell open. He was asking her to answer just like that? As though his proposal of marriage were no more than asking her preference between hamburgers and hot dogs.

"You expect me to just give you a yes or no?" she gasped.

What were you expecting, Hannah, she asked herself wryly. Flowers, music, romance? What a joke. She'd never get that from a man. It was time she faced that fact.

One of his shoulders shrugged negligibly, but on the inside, his heart was a thundering drum. Jess felt as if everything, his and Daniel's whole future, hinged on her answer. "It has to be yes or no. There can't be any inbetweens."

No, Hannah supposed he was right about that. It was either yes or no. Marry him, or tell him goodbye. Still, she wasn't ready for this. It was all too much, too fast.

Incredulous, she stared at him. "I don't—I *can't* give you an answer now! Just like that!"

The breath whooshed out of Jess in a deflating rush. Ever since he'd hung up the phone, he'd been on a tightrope, anticipating her answer. Now she was saying she *couldn't* answer! He wanted to shake her!

"Why not?"

Knowing she couldn't form one sensible word if she continued to look at him, Hannah walked over to a worn armchair.

"Because this is...not normal." She eased down on the edge of the chair and carefully folded her hands in her lap. "A man just doesn't impulsively ask a woman to marry him."

Still standing just inside the door, Jess jammed his fists into the pockets of his jeans. "It isn't on impulse, Hannah. I've thought this through."

She lifted skeptical eyes to his face. "You have?"

Nodding, he walked over to where Hannah sat rigidly on the faded cushion and looked down at her. "I want you to marry me."

Just hearing him say it nearly took her breath away. "Why?"

Frustrated, he swiped a hand over his dark hair. "I told you why! Because of Daniel. I want what's best for my son."

She knew he was being truthful with her and she appreciated his honesty. Still, deep down, the woman part of her was hurt.

Her eyes searched his as she tried to figure out what he was really thinking. "I can't believe you'd go so far as to marry a woman just because your son needs a baby-sitter," she said, sounding faintly disgusted.

"I don't just want a baby-sitter for Daniel," he insisted, wondering what it was going to take to make her say yes, or if he even could. "I want you to be his real mother."

Hannah was stunned. To care for a child was one thing, but being a real mother was entirely something else. Did Jess realize that?

"Jess, that is—" It was incredible, she thought, slowly moving her head back and forth. "I don't know what to say."

Seeing that she was shivering, Jess reached for her hand. "You're cold," he said. "Your coat is damp. Let me take it, and then we'll go to the kitchen where it's warmer."

Hannah allowed him to tug her up from the chair, but she hesitated about removing her coat. She hadn't forgotten how he'd looked at her this morning at the door and she was already unsettled enough.

"I'm not that cold," she insisted.

Ignoring her protest, he pulled the coat from her shoulders and tossed it across the armchair. "You'll get the sniffles wearing that thing for very long."

Even though she was wearing a nightgown and a robe over it, Hannah felt naked without her coat. Instinctively, her arms came up and crossed over her chest in a self-protective gesture.

But in her attempt to hide herself, Hannah only managed to draw Jess's attention from her face to where her arms were pushing her breasts up and out.

So Hannah wasn't thin everywhere, Jess concluded, his eyebrows unconsciously lifting as he took in the enticing shape of her breasts.

Seeing the direction his gaze had taken, Hannah realized what she was doing. Red-faced, she dropped her arms and hurried ahead of him toward the kitchen.

His mind whirling, Jess followed her. What the hell was he doing? If he was going to make this thing work with Hannah, he couldn't be thinking about her breasts or anything else about her body! He couldn't be thinking about her in that way at all!

Entering the kitchen, Hannah took a seat closest to the small gas heater while Jess went to the cabinets and took down two mugs.

"I just made a fresh pot of coffee," he said. "It might help you warm up."

Coffee at midnight? Did this man ever sleep, she wondered. Or were his work hours too unpredictable to give him a normal routine?

"Yes, I'll take a cup. Thank you," she said, telling herself she wouldn't sleep a wink for the remainder of the night, anyway.

After Jess had poured the coffee and taken a seat across from her at the small dinette table, he said, "I guess you never expected me to come out with something like this. I mean, you and me—getting married."

She'd figured the world ending would have been a more likely occurrence than having Jess Malone propose to her. Wrapping her fingers around the warm mug, she glanced over at him. "I'm not so sure you've really thought any of this through. And I can't help but wonder why you're asking me. Surely you know lots of women in Douglas who would be more suitable. Don't you?"

He looked at her, his expression suddenly turning wry. "Oh, I know women down there. I don't know about *lots* of them. But... well, none of them are mother material. Or even wife material, if you know what I mean."

Hannah wasn't naive. She knew exactly what he meant. "I think I do," she said softly, a faint tinge of pink seeping into her cheeks.

Jess saw her embarrassment, but rather than finding it amusing, he felt a little ashamed of himself. Which was crazy of him, he thought. He'd never implied that he lived like a monk. "Look, Hannah," he said, suddenly feeling

the need to explain himself. "The women I know are...
well, they're like me. Just out for a good time. They're not
looking for an emotional commitment and neither am I."

Her eyes widened as she studied his face. He wasn't
looking for an emotional commitment? Just what was he
looking for?

Oh, hell, why had he said that, Jess asked himself. It
hadn't sounded good, even to his own ears. But it was the
truth and now wasn't the time to be humming and haw-
ing.

"I see," she said, the flare of her nostrils telling Jess just
how much she did see.

Fidgeting with the handle on his mug, he said quickly,
"Hannah, it would be stupid of me to try to turn this into
something romantic. Or to try to charm you into saying
yes. We both know that... well, we hardly know each
other."

"That's true," she said, refusing to meet his gaze. "It
would be stupid." She wasn't the sort he would ever want
to *really* marry, she told herself, with an odd pang of regret.

Jess took a sip of coffee and studied her downbent head.
She didn't appear too happy about any of this. But how
did a man tell anything about a woman like Hannah. She
was different. She wasn't to be flirted with or cajoled. She
was too honest, too direct for that kind of thing.

Pushing his fingers through his dark hair, he said, "If
you're worrying about—if you're wondering about—" He
stopped, cursing himself for being so tongue-tied. "Our
marriage would be strictly platonic," he blurted out.

Her head jerked up and her gray eyes met his. Somewhere in the back of her mind, she'd been expecting him
to say such a thing. Still, it hurt to know that she was so—
so undesirable that he wanted to make sure she wouldn't

expect him to perform his husbandly duties. Dear God, was she that bad to look at? Was there something about her that made men think of her as a thing rather than a woman?

Drawing her shoulders up with as much pride as she could muster, she said, "I didn't expect anything else. After all, it's like you said. It would be foolish to look for romance where there is none."

Relieved that she was being so sensible, he nodded eagerly. "That's why I think a marriage between us would be good. We wouldn't have romance or sex getting between us and causing problems. Our attention would be focused on Daniel instead of each other."

Growing up without a father had taught Hannah just how much children need two parents. But to marry a man solely for a child's sake, could she do that?

"I don't know, Jess," Hannah began, doubts shadowing her eyes. "Marriage isn't supposed to be an arrangement."

It was supposed to be loving, giving, needing—sharing your whole life with another person, she thought. What Jess was proposing was the coldest thing she'd ever heard of. And it hurt. Hurt her far more than she wanted to admit.

"It isn't supposed to be a living hell, either. But lots of marriages are nowadays."

Hannah could hardly argue that point. She'd seen several marriages around here slowly crumble over the past few years.

"I know that you're thinking about Daniel," she told him. "And that's good. But what about yourself? Maybe you don't want a real marriage now. But you might later. You might eventually meet a woman you'll fall in love with. Then I'd only be in the way." Hannah looked away from him as she said the last. She was afraid if she didn't he might actually read something on her face, something that would tell him that she would rather be the woman he loved than the woman he was married to.

Hannah be in the way? Jess couldn't imagine it. She made it sound as if she'd be a pile of garbage he'd be forced to walk around. Why would she think that? And for his falling in love, he wanted to throw his head back and laugh. That would be the last thing on earth he would ever let himself do.

But he could hardly tell Hannah such a thing. She'd think he was a coldhearted, cynical bastard. "It doesn't have to be forever," he told her. "Would that make you feel better about things?"

No sex. No love. And when the calendar turned to a certain month, a chosen day, it would be all over. How could any woman feel good about a marriage like that?

Suddenly chilled to the bone, Hannah got up from her chair and went to stand by the heater. "I don't know, Jess. This is all so fast. I can't make a snap decision about this. There are too many things to consider."

In spite of her words, there was something in her voice that gave him hope. "As far as finances are concerned, don't worry about that part. I'll treat you just like any normal wife." He looked at her, his green eyes beseeching. "I'll take care of you, Hannah."

I'll take care of you. Such sweet words when spoken from the heart, she thought. But Jess wasn't speaking from the heart. He was talking about money, food, shelter.

There was a lump in her throat and she didn't know why. She tried her best to swallow it before she spoke. "That's very generous of you, Jess. But I—"

He could hear doubts creeping back into her voice. Quickly, he got up and went over to her. "I wouldn't call it generous, Hannah. Only fair.'' He reached for her hands. They were soft and small and cold as he took them inside his. Jess realized he wanted to warm them as much as he wanted to reassure her.

"I've never lived with anyone. Other than my mother," she confessed, her heart beating rapidly now that he was standing so close, holding her hands as though she were actually someone special. "I don't know if we could even get along well enough to live under the same roof."

A smile spread across his face, a beguiling smile that showed his teeth and dimpled his cheek. "I think we can learn. I might be too messy for you. And you might be too clean for me. But there's always a middle ground somewhere."

She was melting and there didn't seem to be any way she could stop it. The feel of his hands curled tightly around hers made everything feel so good, so right. How could any woman say no when she felt like this? How could she say no to a man like Jess, a man that was looking at her as though he really needed her?

Maybe he didn't love her, she argued. Maybe the marriage wouldn't last that long. But wouldn't it be more than what she had now? Since her mother had passed away, she was virtually alone, other than a few friends she'd made through work and church. She was thirty-three. More than likely, she'd never receive another proposal of marriage. Wouldn't it be better to be Jess's friend-wife than to live alone for the rest of her life?

"How...long would this marriage last?" she asked.

How long? Jess had always believed that when a person said I do, it meant till death do us part. Apparently, Hannah was thinking differently, otherwise she wouldn't be asking. "I don't know," he hedged. "I hadn't thought about it."

She continued to look at him, her expression clearly saying she was waiting on his answer. Jess's mind began to race. He knew he wanted Daniel to have a mother for always, or at the very least, until he was through high school. But maybe it would be asking too much of Hannah to be his wife for that long. On the other hand, he couldn't expect Daniel to get used to having her for a mother, then have her leave because the marriage had run its allotted time.

"Uh…well," he began slowly, "we could make it a trial arrangement for a year. After that, we could see how things are going and talk about what we want to do. How does that sound to you?"

It sounded like a business deal to her. But that's what this whole thing was, she quickly reminded herself. And if she was going to be Jess's wife, she had to remember that.

Suddenly, there was a burning at the back of her eyes. She blinked rapidly, terrified that a tear would brim over and fall onto her cheek for him to see. He wouldn't understand her getting emotional over all of this. She didn't quite understand it herself. "It sounds like this is what you really want."

She couldn't imagine how much he wanted it. "I do. And I hope you do, too," Jess said.

Her gray eyes, which had been carefully focused on the toes of his cowboy boots, now lifted to meet his green ones. "I do want it. So, I guess I'll be your wife, Jess."

She said it so quietly, so solemnly that for a moment Jess didn't realize she was accepting his proposal. Then shock and a wild look of joy exploded across his face.

"You do? You'll marry me?"

The questions came at her in a rush. Hannah nodded in response, then unexpectedly found herself smiling at him.

He seemed so happy about it. As if she really was his love and his heart had been hungering for her answer.

Now that she'd made her decision, she answered with stronger certainty. "I will. So I guess you're going to be getting a wife, and Daniel will be getting a mother."

Elation soared through Jess. Before he realized exactly what he was doing, he tugged Hannah forward and into his arms.

She landed against his muscular chest with a thud and a soft gasp. Instinctively, her hands came up to push herself away, but before she could manage to do more than glance up at him, his mouth swooped down on hers.

Long seconds passed before Jess became aware of what he was doing, and by then he was liking it too much to stop. Hannah's lips were soft, warm and as sweet as nectar from a piece of vine-ripened fruit.

Hannah's senses were spinning out of control. She'd been kissed before. A long time ago. But that memory didn't compare to this very moment in Jess's arms. Her heart was racing like a thing gone mad, her knees were on the verge of buckling and she could think of nothing. Nothing except the warm, firm pressure of his mouth, the feel of his hands on her shoulders, the earthy scent of him rising to her nostrils and filling her head with all sorts of erotic notions.

As abruptly as Jess started the kiss, he ended it. Tearing his mouth away from Hannah's, he stepped back and stared at her as if he wasn't sure which one of them had suddenly lost their minds.

"I—Hannah, I'm sorry," he finally said, his voice husky and apologetic. "I didn't mean to..."

Except for two bright flags of color across her cheek and the deep-kissed pink of her lips, her face was colorless. As though his bold behavior had shocked the blood from her body. Well, Jess could have told her he was feeling pretty shocked himself. But he wouldn't. He had to play this light. After all, it hadn't meant anything. It was nothing more than a little kiss between two friends—who were going to get married.

Too shaken to look at him any longer, Hannah turned away and took several deep breaths. Dear God, she couldn't let him see that his kiss had left her reeling.

"Hannah? Are you all right?"

His fingers touched her hair, then coiled themselves through the shiny strands. A flash fire of currents coursed along Hannah's body.

"Yes. Yes, I'm fine." Was that her voice? She sounded odd, strangled. Swallowing, she forced herself to look over her shoulder and up at him, as though kissing a man was something very natural for her. "Why shouldn't I be?"

He shrugged, his fingers still playing with her hair. It was beautiful, the waves rich-red and silky. Rita Hayworth hair, he mused. Until she pinned it up in a tight knot.

Clearing his throat, he pulled his gaze off her hair and onto her face. "I was afraid I might have scared you. Or offended you with that...uh, kiss." His eyes drifted downward to where her pink mouth was trembling ever so slightly. The sight made Jess want to kiss her all over again, to turn that quiver into a satisfied pout.

"I'm not—" She took another deep breath. "Just forget it, Jess."

From the look on her face, he could tell she was just as shaken as he was. But Jess hardly knew what to do or say to take away the tension that had suddenly sprung up between them. Maybe the best thing he could do was leave it alone. Because he damn well didn't intend to ever repeat what had just happened between them.

"Yeah, you're right," he said softly. "Let's forget it. Let's call it an engagement kiss and leave it at that."

She would leave it at that. Especially when it would probably be the only kiss she'd ever get from him.

Desperate now to put the whole thing behind them, Hannah moved over to the table and picked up her mug.

"I think—it's late," she said jerkily. "I'd better be getting back to my house."

Bemused by her, their kiss and the whole idea that he was going to get married, Jess could only stare at her as she poured her coffee down the sink.

"You're going back to your house?"

Eyebrows lifted, she turned to look at him. There was an odd inflection in his voice. For one wild second, Hannah thought it was the sound of disappointment. "Why, yes. Is something wrong?"

He didn't want her to go. That was the thing that was wrong. She made this house, tomorrow, everything seem brighter. How could that be?

Jess told himself to snap out of this unexpected feeling that had come over him. He needed Hannah for Daniel's sake. Not for his own. Never for his own. He had to remember that.

"Uh—no. Nothing is wrong. I'll come over in the morning and we'll work out the when and where of things. Is that all right with you?"

The business was back in his voice. Hannah squared her shoulders and turned to face him. "That's fine," she said. "Come at eight and I'll have breakfast ready."

"We'll be there."

Jess followed her back to the living room where she jerked on her raincoat without giving him the chance to help her.

"Good night," she said as she walked to the door.

"Good night, Hannah. And . . . thank you."

Pausing, her hand on the doorknob, she glanced over her shoulder at him. They were two people who'd just agreed to get married, yet they were acting more like strangers, she thought.

That's because Jess *is* a stranger, a tiny voice whispered inside her head. You're going to be living with a man you don't even know.

"What are you thanking me for?" she asked.

"For agreeing to become my wife."

His words both hurt and pleased her. "You're welcome, Jess," she said, then quietly let herself out the door.

Chapter Five

Hannah was a woman of strict routine. She never over-slept. She was never late. But this morning, she was guilty of both. It was a quarter to eight and she was just now starting breakfast.

Groggily, she turned the sizzling sausage, then went to fill the coffee machine with grounds and water. She was still in her nightgown and robe and her hair was hanging in a disheveled mess around her face, but there was nothing she could do about that now. Jess and Daniel would be here in fifteen minutes. She didn't have time to do anything about her looks.

Not that she could, anyway, she thought as she switched on the coffee machine. After she'd left Jess last night, she'd been too keyed up to even sit down, much less go to sleep. Her mind had been one great whirling machine, refusing to shut down and turn off all the questions and doubts running through it. Not until a little after dawn this morning, had Hannah finally fallen into an exhausted sleep. However, the rest hadn't been enough to revive her or erase the second thoughts she was having about her promise to marry Jess.

Jess and Daniel arrived on Hannah's doorstep promptly at eight. When she opened the door to let them in, Daniel immediately rushed in and wrapped his arms around her upper legs.

Yesterday, when she'd told the two of them goodbye, she'd thought she'd never see the boy again. Now, to have him greet her in such a loving way warmed her heart.

"Good morning, Hannah," Jess said, smiling at her and then at his son who'd buried his nose in the folds of Hannah's robe.

"Good morning," she said, her eyes skittering from Jess's, then dropping to his son's dark shiny crown. "How are you this morning, Daniel?"

He tilted his head back and gave her a wide, happy smile. "I'm good, Hannah. Did you cook pancakes with blueberries in them?"

Laughing softly, she took his hand and led him toward the kitchen. "No. But I think I'll have something you'll like."

Jess closed the door and followed them. If he'd had any second thoughts about marrying Hannah after she'd left him last night, they were gone now. Seeing Hannah and his son together assured him that he was doing the right thing.

She'd cooked biscuits, milk gravy, sausage and fried eggs. To go along with all that were two flavors of jelly, a jar of honey with a honeycomb in it, coffee, and milk for Daniel.

Daniel was more than curious about the honeycomb, and while they ate, Hannah told him all about the bees and the way they worked. He listened intently, fascinated with the idea that a bug of sorts could make something that tasted so good.

After they finished eating, Daniel went outside to find Oscar. Lingering over their coffee, Hannah and Jess remained at the breakfast table.

"Where did you learn to cook like this? From your mother?"

Embarrassed, Hannah fiddled with the handle of her coffee cup. "No. My mother wasn't much on cooking. Or anything that had to do with home life. She liked going out and excitement."

And from the looks of things, Hannah was the very opposite of Rita Dunbar. Jess wondered if that was intentional on Hannah's part, or if she was just naturally a different type of person than her mother.

"Well, wherever you learned to cook, you did it right. Breakfast was delicious."

"Thank you," she said, her eyes still on her coffee cup.

When she didn't say more, Jess spoke. "I did a lot of thinking after you left last night."

He couldn't have possibly done more thinking than she had. The dark shadows under her eyes could attest to that.

"So did I," she murmured.

"I think we should get married tomorrow."

Her head jerked up. "Tomorrow! That's not possible."

His eyebrows lifted. "It isn't? I'm not sure about the marriage laws here in New Mexico. If there's a waiting period here, we'll drive somewhere where there isn't one."

Hannah quickly shook her head. "I don't mean legally. I mean—it's too soon for me!"

"It is? Why? Surely you weren't wanting a big wedding, or anything, were you?"

Hannah hadn't even thought about the ceremony. She was still trying to get used to the idea of living under the same roof as Jess.

"Er—no. I don't have—" She stopped, not wanting to admit she didn't have the clothes or the funds to have a large wedding. "No. I don't want a big wedding or anything like that."

The relief on his face was obvious. "Well, I think, under the circumstances, a simple civil ceremony will work better for us."

Hannah was a no-frills person. She always had been and she supposed she always would be. So why did it hurt to think she would be getting married without flowers, or even one note of music?

Annoyed with herself for letting sentiment get in the way of practicality, she rose from the table and started gathering the dirty dishes.

"You're right, Jess. Just anything to make it legal. After all, it's not like we're in love or anything."

In love. If it didn't hurt so much, she would have laughed out loud at the thought of Jess Malone ever falling in love with her.

He watched her carry an armful of dishes over to the sink. She seemed offended by something, but he couldn't figure out why. "Then tomorrow shouldn't be too soon. I'll call my superiors today and let them know I need a couple more days off. That will give us a day to get married and another to drive back to Douglas."

Amazed, she turned to look at him. "I couldn't possibly get my things ready to move by then!" Her eyes suddenly narrowed. "Why are you in such a hurry, anyway? Is Daniel's regular baby-sitter going to be gone when you return to Douglas?"

His need to hurry this thing had nothing to do with Louise's leaving. It had everything to do with a deep-seated fear he had that she would change her mind, back out on their agreement and leave him and Daniel alone again.

He got up from the table and went over to her. "Louise will be there for a week or more. But she has nothing to do with my being in a hurry."

Hannah watched him lean his hip into the cabinet counter and fold his arms across his chest. He was wearing a heavy cotton shirt of navy blue and a pair of jeans that had faded to the color of a cornflower.

Somehow, the blue of his clothes made his eyes look that much greener. Their color mesmerized her, as did the width of his shoulders, the leanness of his waist. He was a man who'd been blessed with looks. So why, when he could so obviously pick and choose, was he marrying her? she wondered for the umpteenth time.

Because Daniel wants you, a little voice inside her answered. And being a father meant far more to Jess than being a husband.

"Then why are you—hurrying?" she asked huskily.

"Because it's hard for me to just get time off whenever I want it. If we don't marry now, it might be several weeks before I could get off. Louise will be gone by then."

He had a logical reason for everything, she thought, moving away from him and back to the table.

"Then I guess—I guess I'll do my best to be ready by tomorrow." Methodically, she began scraping the leftovers into an empty plate. "Have you told Daniel yet?"

"No. I was waiting to see if you agreed on getting married tomorrow. Now that you have, I'm going to go find him and give him the good news. He's going to be one happy little boy."

Hannah looked up to see him give her a wink, then start toward the back door. She let out a long sigh. Daniel was going to be happy. But what about her and Jess?

Hannah had worked for Nina Rodriguez for nearly ten years and the two of them had been friends for even longer. It was no doubt, knowing Hannah as well as she did, that the older woman was shocked when Hannah called her later in the day with the news that she was getting married.

"You're getting what?" The older woman gasped the question.

"You didn't hear wrong," Hannah told her. "I'm getting married tomorrow."

"But to whom? You haven't said a word about—who have you been seeing?" she asked in her heavily accented English.

Hannah couldn't bring herself to tell Nina she hadn't been seeing anyone. Suddenly, she didn't want her closest friend in Lordsburg to know her marriage would be a business deal rather than a union of love.

"Someone from my old school days. He's—he moved away a long time ago."

"Do I know him? What's his name?"

"Jess Malone."

There was a gasp. "Hannah! Do you mean the son of Frank? The man who just passed away?"

Hannah leaned her head against the back of the couch and closed her eyes. No doubt everyone who knew her, or Jess, was going to be shocked at their marriage. Hannah wasn't looking forward to hearing it in their voices, or seeing it on their faces. It would only remind her that the marriage wasn't real, and that if it wasn't for Daniel, Jess would have never looked twice at her.

"Yes. That's right. I—uh, of course he came into town because of his father's death. But we—were corresponding long before that."

There was a terribly long pause. Hannah could only imagine what the other woman was thinking. Probably that she was crazy, or lying. "Nina? Are you still there?"

"Yes. I'm thinking, that's all. Are you sure this isn't all too sudden? Jess Malone. If I remember right, he was that wild boy that used to rip through the streets on his motorcycle."

Hannah breathed deeply. "He's not a boy anymore, Nina. He's a grown man and he works for the U.S. Border Patrol in Douglas, Arizona."

"Douglas. Oh my, that means you'll eventually be moving."

Hannah pressed her fingers against her closed eyelids. "That's something I need to talk to you about. Jess wants to get married tomorrow and leave for Douglas the next day. Can you find a replacement for me that quickly?"

"I'm not worried about finding a replacement. Jennifer McClean has been begging me for a job. But I am worried about you, Hannah!" She made a tsking sound with her tongue. "This isn't like you at all. Has that man seduced you with all sorts of promises that he can't or won't keep? Remember Ted? You thought he loved you, too. But he was only out for what he could get from you. That's all."

With a tight grimace on her face, Hannah scooted to the edge of the couch. Nina knew very well that Hannah hadn't forgotten the pain and humiliation she'd suffered from that one brief relationship. But Jess was nothing like Ted, she argued with herself, her gaze drifting to the picture window and the view of the Malone house. No. Hannah needn't worry that Jess was out to seduce her. He'd made it quite clear that love and sex would be the very last thing he'd want from her.

"Jess is nothing like that. Besides, Ted happened years ago when I was very young. I'm a mature woman now, I know better than to naively let some guy talk me into going to bed with him."

"Maybe it did happen a long time ago," Nina conceded. "But I know that you are still carrying the scars from it. Are you sure you know what you're doing this time? How long have you been thinking about getting married, anyway? You haven't even mentioned that you were in love!"

Hannah never lied to anyone about anything. It just wasn't in her nature to be dishonest. But she could hardly explain to Nina that she was going into a loveless marriage. Her friend would never understand. "I've been thinking about it long enough. Besides, how often have you told me that I should find a nice man to settle down with?"

"That's right. I wanted you to find a nice *older* man. One that's settled. One you can be sure of."

Hannah's eyes remained on the Malone house, but she was actually seeing Jess, his green eyes and dark skin, the bright flash of his smile. "You really mean one that I'd have to be helping out of the easy chair after a couple of years of marriage," Hannah said.

"Better than having to knock him off a bar stool," Nina countered with a conviction that spoke from past experiences.

"I don't think I'll have that problem with Jess."

Hannah's friend and employer let out a troubled sigh. "Are you really sure you know what you're getting into, Hannah?"

At this point, Hannah wasn't sure about anything except that tomorrow she was going to become Mrs. Hannah Malone. She would be Jess's wife and Daniel's mother. Wasn't that enough?

"Yes. I'm very sure. I love Jess. And he—" She closed her eyes and swallowed hard. She couldn't bring herself to say that Jess loved her back. That would be taking the lie too far. "He'll be good to me."

Nina let out another sigh, but this time she sounded more resigned than anything. "Then I guess that's all that matters. I only want you to be happy, Hannah. My goodness, you're like a daughter to me."

Yes, Nina was one of the very few true friends Hannah had in Lordsburg. The woman had never shunned her or tried to change her. She'd given her a job and had helped her through the grief of losing her mother. She'd never forget Nina's kindness. "Don't worry, Nina. I'll be happy. I promise."

They talked for a few more minutes before saying their goodbyes. Hannah was relieved once she finally hung up the phone. She already had enough doubts about this whole thing without Nina's filling her with more.

Across the street, Jess shifted the telephone receiver to his other ear. "You heard me right, Dwight. I'm getting married tomorrow. And I want—"

"Married! You said married, Jess! Did someone knock you in the head?"

"Damn it, Dwight, will you shut up and listen? I don't have amnesia, I haven't had a knock on the head, and I'm not delirious with fever."

Jess's friend and co-worker let out a snort of disbelief. "Then why are you getting married? No—no. Don't bother answering that. Just tell me where you found this woman? What did she do to you?''

Jess let out a long breath. He should have expected Dwight to react this way when he heard the news. He knew better than anyone how hurt Jess had been when Michelle had skipped out. He also knew that Jess had vowed never to get involved with another woman. But this was a very different thing, Jess assured himself. He wasn't having a love affair. He was merely getting Daniel a good mother.

''I didn't *find* her anywhere. I already knew Hannah from high school.''

''Oh,'' he said, suddenly thrown by that bit of information. ''Then you really are serious? You're actually getting married?''

Dwight made it sound as if Jess had decided to jump off the edge of the Grand Canyon. ''Yes. Tomorrow. We'll be driving back home Tuesday. Do you think Tracie would mind going over and cleaning up the house for me? I don't want Hannah seeing the mess I left it in.''

''Yeah, yeah, Tracie will be thrilled to do it. She's gonna have a fit when she hears the news. But, buddy, I've got to know what this is all about. You don't even like women that much, except for—''

''Dwight, this thing with Hannah is different,'' Jess interrupted before his friend could get started.

''I've heard that before.''

''Not from me,'' Jess countered.

There was silence, then Dwight said, ''You're right. I haven't heard that from you. I've never heard anything like this from you. But I've got to admit I'm glad the love bug has finally bitten you. You need a woman—''

''Love has nothing to do with this,'' Jess quickly barked at him. ''Hannah is going to be Daniel's mother.''

"What do you mean? Of course she's going to be his mother if she marries you."

Jess scowled, annoyed with his friend for being so damn nosy. What did it matter to Dwight whether Jess was in love with Hannah or not, or whether this marriage was romantic or platonic. "Hannah and I are getting married for Daniel's sake and that's the only reason. You can tell Tracie that if you want, but I'd rather you two didn't bring it up around Hannah. She's—well, she's sensitive. It might be embarrassing for her."

If Dwight had been floored before, he was down for the count now. After long moments passed and the other man didn't make any sort of comeback, Jess very nearly shouted, "Dwight? Damn it, why don't you say something? Are you still there?"

"I think you've lost your mind, buddy. You can't just marry a woman because of Daniel."

"Daniel is my son. I'd do anything for him."

"Apparently."

"What does that mean?"

"Nothing," Dwight answered, then quickly added, "I've got to go. The captain is sending us up to Bisbee. I'll see you Tuesday."

"About the house—"

"Don't worry about it," Dwight assured him. "Tracie will have everything in order. I only hope that you do."

Before Jess could ask him to explain that remark, Dwight had hung up.

Cursing to himself, Jess dropped the receiver onto its hook. What was his friend expecting out of him, anyway, he wondered as he leaned his head against the couch cushions and closed his eyes. There wasn't any cause for Dwight to sound so disapproving. Hell, it wasn't as if Jess was going to damage Hannah by marrying her!

Would Dwight think better of the marriage if Jess were madly in love with Hannah? The idea put a bitter twist on Jess's mouth. He didn't have to be in love to make Daniel happy. And as far as Jess was concerned, that was all that mattered to him.

Opening his eyes, he saw that Daniel had stopped pushing his toy dump truck across the floor and was studying him intently.

"Are you sick, Daddy?"

Jess shook his head to dispel the troubled look on Daniel's face. "No, son. I'm fine. In fact, I think it's time for us to go over and help Hannah pack her things. Are you ready?"

Just the mention of Hannah's name put a sparkle in Daniel's eyes. "Yea!" he exclaimed, then suddenly his little face went somber. "Daddy, is Hannah really going to be my mommy?"

Even though Jess had explained this morning that he was going to marry Hannah and that she would be moving to Douglas with them, the child still seemed uncertain about the whole thing, as though it was all too good to be real.

Jess pulled his son onto his lap and gently passed his hand over Daniel's dark hair. "Yes, Daniel. Hannah really is going to be your mommy."

"Will she live in our house? With us?"

Jess nodded and some of the doubts disappeared from Daniel's face. "Will she be there when I wake up?"

"She sure will. She'll even fix your breakfast."

Liking what he was hearing, Daniel gave his father a big grin. "And will she be there when I take a bath and go to bed?"

Jess smiled, his heart full of love as he looked at his son. "Yes, she'll be there then, too."

"For always? Do you promise she'll be there for always?" Daniel persisted.

The hopeful innocence on Daniel's face tore at him and he knew the only thing he could say was yes. He'd worry later about making the promise come true.

Hugging Daniel fiercely to his chest, he murmured against the top of the child's head, "I promise, son. Hannah will always be with us."

"I'm not really sure about what to take with me," Hannah said a little later that evening as she and Jess filled cardboard boxes with clothing.

Jess glanced around the small bedroom. Where he had simple blinds covering his windows at home, Hannah had ruffled priscillas. Instead of a corded bedspread, she had a flowered comforter with several brightly covered pillows that matched. The bedstead was white ironwork. Obviously an antique that had been lovingly restored. There was a cedar chest at the foot. At the head was a nightstand with an old hurricane lamp atop it. Next to it was a small basket full of dried rose petals.

There was a part of her in these things, this room, and it sent a strange surge of feeling through him to know that she was giving it all up for him. And Daniel.

Without conscious thought, his eyes drifted back to the bed and for one wild second, he imagined what Hannah would look like lying there against the rose-printed sheets and lace-edged pillows. He could almost see the fan of her red hair, the startling white contrast of her naked skin. She would be beautiful. Somehow, he knew that.

"Jess? Jess, is something wrong?"

Her voice jolted him back to reality. A dull flush on his face, he looked away from the bed and over to her. "If you—if you'd rather have your own bedroom furniture, we can rent a trailer," he said.

His gesture surprised her. She hadn't expected him to be so thoughtful. "That isn't necessary," she assured him as she looked around her bedroom. "I'm sure the furniture you have will be fine. And maybe it will help rent this place if I leave all the furnishings here."

One dark eyebrow inched upward. "You're not going to put this house up for sale?"

Hannah shook her head. "No. I—well, Mother and I sacrificed for years to pay for this house. I really hate to get rid of it." She didn't add that she would obviously need it once their marriage ended.

Daniel, unaware of the sacrifices the two adults were about to make for him, raced around the room, picking up everything from photos to hairbrushes.

"Take this, too, Hannah," he said, wagging a little stuffed kitten over to the foot of the bed. "I like him."

Hannah took the stuffed animal from Daniel. "I don't know, Daniel. There might not be room for him."

Jess watched her absently stroke the toy between the ears. There was an odd, almost pained look on her face and he wondered what was bothering her.

"The toy came from someone special?" he asked.

She glanced at him briefly, then back to the kitten in her hands. "Yes. I guess you could say that."

Several moments passed. Jess wanted to ask her to explain, but he knew he had no right. He wasn't a lover who was privy to her private thoughts. But just for a moment, when her eyes had shadowed over, the need to *really* know her had tugged at him.

Suddenly, she looked up at him. "My father gave it to me when I was very small. Or so my mother said."

"You don't sound very sure of that."

She glanced away from him, but not before Jess saw the bitter twist to her lips. "Sometimes I'm not even sure I ever had a father."

"You never knew him at all?" Jess prompted, surprised at how curious he was to know this woman who was to become his wife.

Hannah shook her head, then gave him a sidelong glance. "He and my mother never married. Though she said they lived together until I was about two years old. After that, he got the wanderlust—or something. Mother was always vague about that part of it." Shrugging, Hannah looked down at the toy kitten in her hands. "Anyway, he left and she never heard from him again."

Jess didn't know what to say. But he wished he did. He'd like more than anything to be able to take away the sadness on her face.

"I guess neither one of us had much in the way of parents," he said, then wondered if he was a little crazy for thinking that two people, both from broken homes, could be good parents to Daniel.

Hannah didn't reply. There wasn't much need to reiterate the obvious. Instead, she handed the stuffed animal back to Daniel. "I think it's time I gave this kitten a new home. Would you like to have him, Daniel?"

"Yeah! Thanks, Hannah!" Daniel shouted happily, then raced for the door. "I'm gonna go put him in the pickup so I won't forget him."

Once Daniel disappeared out the door, Jess moved closer to Hannah "You didn't have to do that," he said quietly. "That toy was a keepsake."

Hannah shook her head. "I want Daniel to have it." She looked up at him and her heart began to hammer at his closeness. Dear Lord, she silently prayed, how was she ever going to get used to living with this man? How could she be near him like this, hear his voice, rest her eyes on his face and not lose her heart to him?

"Hannah? What's the matter?" Jess asked as the pensive expression on her face turned to a troubled one.

Quickly, she turned away from him and walked over to an old Hollywood-style dresser. Once there, she picked up a box of hair ribbons, but from the way her hands were shaking, anyone would have thought it was a bomb, instead.

"I don't—" She gripped the small box. "I guess I'm afraid, Jess," she said after a moment, her voice low and tremulous.

He studied her downbent head, the exposed nape of her neck, the slender figure she made in the dark skirt and white blouse she was wearing. She seemed so very fragile and even more vulnerable. She was so different from what he was used to. She brought out things in him he'd rather not be feeling. Like the need to go to her, put his arms around her and assure her that everything would be all right.

"Of me?" he wanted to know.

Her back still to him, she shook her head. "No. It's—just—"

The tremor in her voice had him moving across the room to her. Before he could stop himself, he put his hands on her shoulders. "Don't be afraid, Hannah," he murmured gently. "Everything will work out. Why, after a few days, you won't even miss this place."

Missing this place was the last thing Hannah was worried about. She was desperately afraid of falling in love with him. But she could hardly tell him that. He'd more than likely laugh his head off.

"You're probably right."

"I'm sure I'm right. Douglas might not be heaven but it damn sure isn't hell." He squeezed her shoulders and she could hear a smile in his voice when he spoke again. "Although it might seem like it, come July."

Even though his hands were the only things touching her, Hannah was acutely aware of the length of his body just inches behind her, the heat of him, the scent of him. And for a moment, all she could think about was how it would feel to lean into him. How would it be if his arms came around her, his hands slid slowly upward until they were cupping her breasts?

"...trying to back out on me, are you?"

What had he been saying? Something about backing out? Dear God, he was already making her crazy! How could she be thinking such erotic, wanton thoughts?

Desperately, she moved from beneath his hands and drew in a long breath. "No—I—" She whirled, her gaze seeking and finding his. "I'm not going to back out on you."

Something in her eyes caused his gaze to slip down her throat, then even farther to where her collar folded back against her breasts. He could see that she was breathing as if she'd been running. And his heart, Jess realized, was a quick thud, thud, thud in his chest. Almost as though he'd been chasing her. Which was crazy, he thought wildly. Hannah wasn't a woman to be chased. So he'd kissed her once. That didn't mean he wanted to strip her of those matronly clothes and make love to her on the bedroom floor!

"That's good. I—"

Suddenly Daniel trotted into the room, this time carrying Oscar. "Can I put Oscar in the pickup, too, Daddy? Are we ready to go home now?"

Home. The word jolted Jess like a current of electricity. Home had always been just him and Daniel. But now, instead of the two of them, it would be the three of them.

Then, before he knew their intention, his eyes had gone back to Hannah, and as he looked at her tender face, he knew that it was too late to change anything. She was going to become a part of their lives. For now. Maybe forever.

Chapter Six

The highway they were traveling was flat, straight and monotonous, the scenery little more than sand, sage and half-dead yucca, yet Hannah had stared out the window for more than an hour now. In fact, since they'd left New Mexico and crossed into Arizona, Hannah had said very little to Jess.

He glanced at her again, hoping the melancholy look he'd seen on her face a few miles back had disappeared. He didn't want her to be sad about leaving Lordsburg. Damn it, what was back there for her to miss? Her mother's grave? An old house filled with sad memories? Surely a life with him and Daniel would be better for her than that, he thought.

"Hannah? Are you okay? Do you need for me to stop... er... at the next rest area?"

She turned her head toward him. "I'm fine, Jess. Is it much farther?"

NO COST! NO OBLIGATION TO BUY!
NO PURCHASE NECESSARY!

PLAY "LUCKY 7"
AND GET FIVE FREE GIFTS!
HOW TO PLAY:

1. With a coin, carefully scratch off the silver box at the right. Then check the claim chart to see what we have for you—FREE BOOKS and a gift—ALL YOURS! ALL FREE!

2. Send back this card and you'll receive brand-new Silhouette Romance™ novels. These books have a cover price of $2.75 each, but they are yours to keep absolutely free.

3. There's no catch. You're under no obligation to buy anything. We charge nothing—ZERO—for your first shipment. And you don't have to make any minimum number of purchases—not even one!

4. The fact is thousands of readers enjoy receiving books by mail from the Silhouette Reader Service™ months before they're available in stores. They like the convenience of home delivery and they love our discount prices!

5. We hope that after receiving your free books you'll want to remain a subscriber. But the choice is yours—to continue or cancel, anytime at all! So why not take us up on our invitation, with no risk of any kind. You'll be glad you did!

This lovely heart-shaped box is richly detailed with cut-glass decorations, perfect for holding a precious memento or keepsake—and it's yours absolutely free when you accept our no-risk offer.

PLAY "LUCKY 7"

**Just scratch off the silver box with a coin.
Then check below to see the gifts you get.**

YES! I have scratched off the silver box. Please send me all the gifts for which I qualify. I understand I am under no obligation to purchase any books, as explained on the back and on the opposite page.

215 CIS ANWZ
(U-SIL-R-07/94)

NAME

ADDRESS   APT.

CITY   STATE   ZIP

 WORTH FOUR FREE BOOKS PLUS A FREE HEART-SHAPED CURIO BOX

 WORTH THREE FREE BOOKS

 WORTH TWO FREE BOOKS

WORTH ONE FREE BOOK

THE SILHOUETTE READER SERVICE™: HERE'S HOW IT WORKS

Accepting free books places you under no obligation to buy anything. You may keep the books and gift and return the shipping statement marked "cancel". If you do not cancel, about a month later we'll send you 6 additional novels, and bill you just $2.19 each plus 25¢ delivery and applicable sales tax, if any.* That's the complete price, and—compared to cover prices of $2.75 each—quite a bargain! You may cancel at any time, but if you choose to continue, every month we'll send you 6 more books, which you may either purchase at the discount price ...or return at our expense and cancel your subscription.

*Terms and prices subject to change without notice. Sales tax applicable in N.Y.

If offer card is missing, write to: Silhouette Reader Service, 3010 Walden Ave., P.O. Box 1867, Buffalo, NY 14269-1867

BUSINESS REPLY MAIL
FIRST CLASS MAIL   PERMIT NO. 717   BUFFALO, NY

POSTAGE WILL BE PAID BY ADDRESSEE

SILHOUETTE READER SERVICE
3010 WALDEN AVE
PO BOX 1867
BUFFALO NY 14240-9952

NO POSTAGE
NECESSARY
IF MAILED
IN THE
UNITED STATES

Jess glanced at his watch. "We'll be home in about twenty minutes."

Nodding, she returned her attention to the scenery passing her window, but her eyes weren't really seeing the thorny cacti and scrubby sage. Jess was taking her home. His home. And soon to be her home. It was still so hard to believe that she was his wife now.

Her eyes slipped away from the passing scenery and down to her hand. The thin gold band encircling her finger felt strange. She'd never worn a ring of any sort, which made her doubly aware of the weight of the cool metal against her skin. It was a constant reminder that her life had drastically changed since yesterday.

This morning, Hannah had been taken by complete surprise when, prompted by the judge, Jess had pulled the ring out of his pocket and slipped it onto her finger. She hadn't expected the ring, nor the small bouquet of pink rosebuds he'd pressed into her hand before the ceremony.

To Hannah, the ring and the flowers were romantic symbols. So why had Jess bothered to give them to her? After worrying the question around in her head all afternoon, she'd finally told herself to let it go. It wouldn't do for her to start weaving romantic notions about Jess. Not today or any day after.

Finally, she decided he'd probably given her the ring because his friends and acquaintances would think it odd if she didn't have one. As for the flowers, well, she put that down to niceness. Nothing more.

Glancing down at Daniel, where he lay between them on the seat, she saw that he was still sound asleep. Hannah missed his chatter, his questions and the way he sidled up to her as though he already instinctively knew that she loved him. He was her son now. Hers and Jess's.

As if with a will of their own, Hannah's eyes lifted from Daniel to his father. They traveled slowly over each feature of his face, down to where his rich brown hair waved against the back of his neck, then on to his broad shoulders, his arms and finally to his lean tanned hands upon the steering wheel.

Before they'd left Lordsburg, he'd changed his pleated trousers and white shirt for blue jeans and a red sweatshirt trimmed with a gray collar. The casual clothes suited his tall, muscular body. She figured Jess would look good in any sort of clothes—or out of them.

Dear God, what was she doing now? She'd only been married a few hours and already she was thinking about Jess naked.

To reprimand herself for the carnal thought, she jerked her eyes straight ahead and off her new husband. To look at him was both thrilling and painful, she realized, and very addictive.

"Jess?"

"Hmm?"

"I wonder—uh, well, what will you tell your friends? About us, I mean."

The question had Jess looking across the seat to Hannah, but even before he did, he could see her in his mind. She still looked as she had this morning when she'd stood beside him and said their marriage vows. She was wearing light blue, the skirt long and full, the top ruffled at the throat and cuffs. Her red hair was twisted into a loose French pleat, and tiny pearls adorned her earlobes. She looked nice. He hadn't told her so, but he'd been thinking it.

"What is there to tell, except that we're married?" He glanced at the road, then back at her. "And as for the nature of our marriage, I don't think anyone will be crass enough to ask us whether we have sex or not."

Heat flashed red across her cheeks and she quickly darted a glance at Daniel to make sure that he was still asleep.

"I guess you're right," she murmured. "But you know how people are—the innuendos they can make. I didn't know if you—"

She could feel his gaze upon her face, and just knowing he was looking at her so intently left her breath and the rest of her words lodged in her throat.

"If I what?" he prompted.

She shifted awkwardly on the seat. "If you—plan to explain the real reason we got married."

Jess's eyes slanted downward to her lap where she still held the nosegay of roses he'd given her this morning. Her forefinger was gently tracing each pink bud as though they had become precious to her. The sight bothered him. He didn't want her getting sentimental.

"Do you want me to explain the real reason?" he asked.

Hannah kept her eyes on the flowers in her lap. "I told my boss—well, I implied to her that we got married for all the usual reasons. I hope that doesn't bother you."

Several moments passed and he didn't say anything. Hannah looked up at him to see if there was anything on his face that might tell her what he was feeling.

"Why should it?" he finally asked. "I don't even know the woman."

His words were clipped as though he was annoyed, perhaps even bored with the subject of their marriage. Hannah found herself feeling a little hurt by his attitude. Even so, she was determined to act as though she were as indifferent about it as he was.

"You're right. And since I don't know your friends, I suppose it's foolish of me to wonder what they might think about us." She shot him a daring look. "Or do you have that many friends?"

"I have a few," he answered dryly, then releasing a long, impatient breath, he glanced over at her. "About our marriage—well, I've already phoned my best friend and told him the real reason we're married. But as for the rest—I—"

Suddenly, the rest of his sentence was forgotten. How could a woman look sweet and sexy at the same time, he wondered. What was it in her clear gray eyes that made him want to promise her anything?

"Yes?" she prompted when he failed to go on.

Jess swallowed hard, then jerked his gaze back onto the highway.

"I think it might be best if we let the rest of them draw their own conclusions about us."

Hannah was relieved. She hadn't wanted his friends looking at her as though she were the hired help. But what about him? Would it bother him to have people think he'd chosen a woman like her for a lifelong mate?

"Thank you, Jess. And, uh, don't worry, I won't expect you to act, er, affectionate or anything out in public just to prove a point."

Frowning, Jess glanced at his sleeping son. He'd heard or read more than once that a child needed to see physical affection exchanged between his parents. Well, he thought a little ruefully, he couldn't give him that, but at least he'd given him a mother.

"You're right," Jess said woodenly. "It would be a phony act if we attempted to behave like true newlyweds."

Hannah clutched the nosegay even tighter and stared out at the passing desert. It was a lonely land they were traveling through, and she couldn't help thinking how well it matched the emptiness in her heart.

Jess's home was an old frame house located on the edge of town. The yard was large and surrounded by chain-link fence. Hannah noticed that as in Lordsburg, trees seem to be equally scarce in Douglas. However, there was one huge cottonwood standing near the house. It shaded a swing set, a sandpile and a part of the front porch that ran the length of the house.

"Well, this is it," Jess told Hannah as he pulled the pickup beneath a carport and cut the engine. "It's nothing fancy, but it's home to me and Daniel."

"It's very nice," she said and meant it. The house had obviously been well kept through the years. The lapped-board siding gleamed with fresh white paint, as did the loden green trim around the windows and the porch. There were no flowers or rosebushes on the lawn, but the grass was thick and green and freshly mown, quite a pleasant change from the rocks and scrubby plants that had been her yard in Lordsburg.

Daniel quickly hopped to his feet and nudged Hannah to open the door. "C'mon, Hannah! Let's get Oscar out of his cage and Albert, too!"

"You'd better take Oscar into the house to let him loose," Jess told his son. "We don't know what Peanuts might do about having a cat share his yard. And don't mess with that cockatoo until Hannah or I can help you. We'll have to put him in the house, too."

"Okay, Daddy."

Hannah opened the pickup door and Daniel quickly scrambled over her legs and down to the ground. Before she followed, she glanced uncertainly at Jess. "Are you sure that's all right? You probably haven't had a cat in the house before. Or a bird, either, for that matter."

He shrugged, then grinned. "No. But we've had worse things in there. Like horned toads and Gila monsters. A lazy tomcat couldn't be any worse. Or a bird that won't talk."

"I'm glad," she said. "I wouldn't want either one of them to be trouble."

She was trying to smile back at him, but Jess could tell her lips were trembling with the effort. She looked uncertain and wary as if coming to live with him was the most frightening thing she'd ever had to face in her life.

As Jess looked at her, something stirred inside him, some emotion he'd never felt, nor could explain or define. Before he realized what he was doing, he reached across the seat and squeezed her hand in his. The wedding ring he'd placed on her finger this morning pressed against his palm. Oddly enough, the feel of it reassured him.

This woman was his wife now. She wouldn't leave him and Daniel. The ring on her finger proved she wasn't like Michelle. He had to believe that.

"Don't worry about the pets, Hannah," he said softly. "Don't worry about anything. This is your home. And we're going to be fine together."

She knew Jess was trying to reassure her, but for some reason, his gentle words brought a knot of emotion to her throat. Since men had always been indifferent to her, it overwhelmed her to have Jess treat her as if she mattered.

Several long moments passed before she could swallow enough of the burning lump in her throat to speak. "I'll do my best to be a good mother to Daniel. I already love him as if he were my own. And I'll be a good wife, too. I can cook most anything. And I'm not that messy. I don't ever spend money unless I have to. And I'll keep—''

Suddenly, the tears were coming fast and hard, choking off the rest of her words.

The sight was like a knife in Jess's chest and he did the only thing he knew to do. Slowly, his arms moved around her, tugged her closer until her head was resting against his chest.

"My goodness, Hannah," he said huskily. "You're fretting for nothing. I'm not worried about any of those things. Not worried one little bit."

Her only response was to grip his shoulders and bury her face deeper in the front of his sweatshirt. Sobs shook her slender body and instinctively Jess tightened his arms around her, and pressed his cheek against the top of her head.

Her red hair was coarse-textured, but surprisingly soft against his skin. It smelled like lavender and the faint scent filled his nostrils. He'd never held a woman to simply comfort her. Especially not one who didn't smell of hair spray, cigarettes and beer.

It didn't make sense, he thought, but holding Hannah like this made him feel like a man. More of a man than he'd ever felt in his life. "You're not sorry you married me, are you?"

She shook her head, then after a moment, she lifted her face from his chest and looked at him through blurry eyes. "Lordsburg is the only home I can ever remember having," she said, her voice a low quiver. "And I don't know all that much about you."

With awkward tenderness, his fingers wiped the tears from her cheeks. "I don't really know a whole lot about you, either." His fist came up beneath her chin and gently lifted her face to his. "But what we don't know about each other, we'll learn."

He smiled at her then, and Hannah felt a part of her begin to melt. How could she regret marrying this man? He was all she'd ever dreamed about.

She sniffed, then gave him the best smile she could. "Then you're not sorry you married me?"

Sorry? No, he was glad he'd married Hannah, he realized as he looked into her liquid gray eyes. Daniel was happier than Jess had ever seen him. And knowing his son was happy made Jess a contented man.

"Of course I'm not sorry," he told her. "You're a good woman, Hannah. Any man would be lucky to have you for a wife. Including me."

The house was much larger than Hannah had expected. The walls were all white, the floors hardwood, except for the kitchen, which was covered with shiny linoleum printed to look like creek gravel. The furniture was mostly new and in an odd assortment of styles, as though it had been chosen for comfort and durability more than anything else. The only thing she saw on the walls was a calendar hanging by the refrigerator in the kitchen. It was scribbled on here and there with three- or four-word notes that she could only guess pertained to Jess's job.

After they'd carried everything in from the truck and got the pets settled, the first thing Jess did was show her where he kept his rifle and his pistol—when he wasn't wearing it at work—locked away in a metal chest in his bedroom closet. In case anyone ever tried to break in while he was away, he told her.

Hannah had never touched a gun of any sort in her life, but she decided she'd wait until later to tell him that. She'd already broken down and cried in front of him. She didn't want him thinking she was a helpless female, right off the bat.

After showing her the gun cabinet, he took her to a utility room at the back of the house. On the wall above the washer and dryer was an electrical breaker box. He showed her how to switch the breakers if a fuse should blow and how to turn off the electricity completely if the need ever arose. Then he took her outside and pointed out the water meter and where to turn the valve if a leak should ever happen and he wasn't at home to take care of it.

Hannah listened closely to all his instructions and nodded each time he asked her if she understood. But inwardly, she was wondering if any other woman had spent the evening of her wedding day looking at breaker boxes and water meters.

Still, she wasn't about to start feeling sorry for herself. Jess hadn't promised her anything but her day-to-day needs and a place to call home.

That night after she'd put Daniel and herself to bed, the telephone rang. As Hannah lay in the dark, staring at the strange walls of her bedroom, she wondered who was calling at such a late hour. A woman, perhaps? Jess had intimated that he had girlfriends. Would he still see them now that he was married? She knew she didn't have any emotional or physical ties on her husband. But she wanted him to be faithful, even if their marriage was in name only.

She was still thinking about it when a knock sounded on her bedroom door.

Clutching the sheet against her breast, she called, "Come in."

The door opened and light from the hallway spilled into the room.

"Hannah?" Jess questioned softly.

She raised herself on her elbow as Jess stepped into the room. "Yes," she answered warily.

He moved toward the bed and Hannah's heart thumped crazily against her breast. What was she afraid of? After all, this man was her husband. Idiot, she chided herself, he isn't here for anything like that. Get it out of your head.

"I have to go to work," he said.

Hannah sat up and turned on the bedside lamp. Immediately, she noticed he was dressed in a khaki-colored uniform with a patch on the arm that read U.S. Border Patrol.

"But you haven't had any sleep!" she exclaimed, her eyes wide with disbelief. "How can you work without any rest?"

Jess wasn't used to having anyone show concern for him. To have Hannah doing so left him with a feeling he didn't understand at all.

"I'm used to it," he mumbled, passing his gun belt from one hand to the other.

Hannah wanted to remind him that it was his wedding night. But then, it wasn't as if he were being torn away from a night of passion, she told herself. "When will you be back?" she asked.

"Probably midmorning, unless something unexpected comes up."

He reached around to his hip pocket and pulled out a leather wallet. While he rifled through its contents, Hannah's eyes roamed over him. She admired the way his dark hair waved neatly away from his forehead and the way his green khaki shirt emphasized his broad shoulders and lean waist. He was so big, she thought, so handsome, so utterly male that merely having him stand here in her bedroom left her almost breathless.

"Here," he said, handing her several bills. "Use this for groceries and whatever else you might need."

Hannah stared at him in total surprise. She hadn't expected him to just casually hand her a wad of money and tell her to spend it for whatever.

She reached to take the money and forgot that she was supposed to be gripping the sheet against her throat. It slid down to her waist, exposing her thin cotton nightgown.

Jess stared. He couldn't help himself. Her bare skin was the color of rich cream and just as smooth. He could see the shape of her firm rounded breasts, the dark rigid circles of her nipples pressing against the soft cotton.

Hannah put the folded bills on the nightstand. "Jess?"

Swallowing hard, he tried to make his eyes look elsewhere. "Uh, yeah. Is that not enough?"

She turned away from the nightstand to see Jess staring at her. Hot color swept up her throat and over her face and she yanked the sheet up beneath her chin.

"I—um—no. That's not—it's plenty of money," she finally managed to say. Dear Lord, what was he thinking? That she was deliberately trying to seduce him?

"Good. I'll see you tomorrow." He took two quick steps backward. "And don't worry about Daniel. Just treat him like he was your own. 'Cause he is now." He took two more steps, then made a dive toward the door.

"Jess?"

Breathing deeply, he forced himself to turn around, but even then he couldn't quite meet her eyes. "I've got to go, Hannah," he said, his voice unusually husky.

"I know," she said, both flustered and annoyed with him, but not really understanding why. "I was just wondering—how do I get to the grocery store?"

Jess was glad he was standing in the shadowed space at the end of the bed, otherwise she would probably see the flush of embarrassment on his face.

"Well, I'll be damned, Hannah," he said with sudden insight. "We're going to have to get you a car."

"A car? No—"

He interrupted before she could put up any sort of argument. "Just go across the street and tell Louise I said to let you use her car. She won't care, she hardly ever drives the thing."

He started out of the room.

She called after him. "But Jess—"

"Good night, Hannah."

His voice came from down the hallway and Hannah knew he was gone. She fell back against the pillow and stared up at the ceiling.

Living with Jess was going to be much harder than she'd ever imagined. She'd been in his home, no, *their* home, she corrected herself, less than a day and already she was thinking about him as a man. A real husband.

And that would never do.

Chapter Seven

Daniel was up early the next morning, and because he didn't seem that surprised to find his father gone, Hannah concluded that Jess's leaving in the night must be a common occurrence. She also decided that cooking and buying groceries was something Jess put off as often as he could.

The only thing she could find in the way of breakfast food was instant oatmeal without milk, instant orange drink and a half-eaten bag of chocolate chip cookies. Hannah didn't like any of the choices and knew she desperately needed to get to the grocery store. But the thought of going across the street to ask a stranger if she could borrow her car was ridiculous. She didn't care what Jess had told her.

After they'd eaten a little of the oatmeal and more of the cookies, she carried a second cup of coffee out to the porch to watch Daniel while he played in his sandpile.

Since Douglas was on the Mexican border and even far-ther south than Lordsburg, she supposed the weather stayed warm most of the time. Even though it was January, her denim skirt and long-sleeved blouse were perfectly comfortable in the morning sunshine.

Hannah had finished her coffee and was pushing Daniel on his swing, when a small dark car pulled into the driveway. She eyed it cautiously.

"That's Tracie," Daniel announced before Hannah had time to ask. "She knows my daddy and me."

In what capacity, Hannah wondered as she watched the petite blonde climb out of the car.

"Hello," she called with a smile and a wave.

Hannah smiled tentatively back at her. "Hello," she replied, when the woman was within a few steps of her and Daniel.

"I'm Tracie Towson," she quickly introduced herself. "My husband, Dwight, works with Jess. You've got to be Hannah."

Hannah nodded, but her expression said she was clearly at a loss.

Tracie laughed, and Hannah, who rarely found much to laugh about, thought it was a very happy sound.

"Jess called Dwight and told him about your marriage. Congratulations," she said with a bright smile as she reached to clasp Hannah's hand. "You don't know how happy I was to hear that Jess had finally found himself a wife."

"Thank you," Hannah said, surprised at the woman's sincerity. She'd expected Jess's friends to view her as an odd stray he'd picked up somewhere, or not much more than that.

"Hannah's my mommy now," Daniel exclaimed, hopping down from the swing and possessively grabbing on to a fold of Hannah's denim skirt.

Tracie's gaze went keenly from child to new mother, then back again. "I know, tiger. That's really nice."

Hannah self-consciously patted the knot of hair at the back of her head. She knew she probably looked strange to Tracie, who was dressed stylishly in a blue cotton jumpsuit. Her blond hair was bobbed, her face enhanced with makeup. She was chic and cute and everything Hannah wasn't.

"Would you like to come in for coffee?" Hannah asked.

"I'd love to. Although I guess I should apologize for showing up uninvited. But I was just dying to meet you, and since I knew Jess was at work, I drove over. I hope you don't mind," she chattered as the three of them trooped into the house.

"No. Of course not," Hannah assured her. "I want to meet Jess's friends."

Daniel went to his room to play and the women went to the kitchen, where Hannah quickly put on a fresh pot of coffee to brew. While she worked, Tracie took a seat at the dining table.

"Did you know Jess's father?" she asked, watching Hannah take cups and saucers from the cabinet.

Hannah carried the dishes over to the table. "I lived across the street from him for years. But I didn't know him that well. He wasn't much of a socializer."

Tracie's face puckered with a frown. "Dwight and I never met the man. As far as we know, he never came down here to visit his son. Jess has been real torn up about his dad. Especially this last year when the man's health really began to deteriorate. Jess tried every way he could to help him. Even had professional health people go in and try, but none of it did any good.''

Hannah remembered the day of the funeral and how bitter and angry Jess had seemed about his father's dying. She hoped she never saw him in that much pain again.

"I don't think Frank Malone wanted to be helped," Hannah told her.

"I think you're right," Tracie said with a somber nod, then suddenly smiled. "So you knew Jess from before?" she asked brightly.

Hannah nodded, unaware of the dreamy-like curve to her lips. "We were neighbors and went to the same school."

Tracie laughed mischievously. "I'll bet you could tell some good tales on him.

Hannah shrugged. "Not really," she said, feeling a dull flush cross her cheeks. "I...wasn't, well, I wasn't in Jess's circle of friends back then."

Nor was she now, Hannah thought as she looked at the vivacious woman across from her. Not that she didn't want to be a part of that circle. For as long as she could remember, she'd wished and wanted to be like other girls, and as she'd grown older, like other women. But for just as long, there'd been a deep fear inside Hannah, one that made her hide behind plain clothes and nondescript hairstyles. Her mother had been beautiful, but she'd also been gossiped about. She'd been hurt and rejected by men, left to raise a child on her own. More than anything, Hannah didn't want to make the same mistakes her mother had made, but she'd never been able to explain that to anyone. So she let them think what they wanted about her appearance.

Tracie must have picked up on her feelings because the next thing she said was, "I don't mean this unkindly,

Hannah, but I've just got to tell you that—you're nothing like what I expected you to be.''

Hannah looked at her. "You mean because I'm so plain," she said frankly.

Tracie gasped, then quickly shook her head with embarrassment. "No! I didn't mean that all! You're just more . . . reserved than what, well, some of Jess's old girlfriends.''

Hannah wanted to point out to Tracie that she'd never been Jess's girlfriend, but since she didn't really know how much this woman knew about the situation, she decided to stay quiet. Let them draw their own conclusions about us, Jess had said.

"I can imagine," Hannah said. "In high school, he always went out with the prettiest girls, and I doubt any of them ever told him no—to anything.''

And, given the chance, she would have probably been the same, Hannah realized with a touch of ruefulness.

"And you had a crush on him?"

Tracie's voice brought Hannah out of her memories with a jolt and she looked with widened eyes at the other woman. "I—what makes you say that?"

Tracie smiled gently. "Something on your face told me."

Hannah let out a long sigh, then went after the coffee, which had finally quit dripping.

"I guess I did have a crush on him. He was really the only boy in school brave enough to talk to me."

Tracie laughed. "Brave enough? Why, were you the class hellion?''

Back at the table, Hannah smiled wanly as she poured the coffee. "No, the class nerd. But I always liked Jess. He was sort of like me. He didn't have a mother. And I didn't have a father. And he was different. Not in a strange way, like me. But different, like a rebel, I guess. I could relate to that in high school. And now I still—I—''

She broke off, shocked that she'd been about to say that she still loved Jess. Dear God, when had she started likening her feelings for Jess to love? Way back then? Just today?

Disturbed at how far her thoughts had taken her, Hannah sank weakly into her chair. Tracie quickly reached across the wooden tabletop and gave Hannah's hand an encouraging squeeze.

''I know. You still care about Jess,'' she said softly.

Hannah nodded as an unexpected lump filled her throat. What was happening to her, she wondered desperately. She'd been more emotional these past few days than in her whole life. Is that what a man can do to a woman? If so, maybe she'd been wise to avoid them all these years.

Tracie gave Hannah's hand another squeeze. ''You know, Hannah, I want us to be more than acquaintances. I want us to be good friends. That's why I'm going to be honest with you.''

Hannah looked at her a little warily and Tracie went on, ''Jess told Dwight about your marriage. I mean, the real reason that he married you. But I think that maybe you married him for a different reason. Am I right?''

Hannah glanced down at her cooling coffee. ''I love Daniel. He's a wonderful little boy. And I've always wanted a child. Marrying Jess seemed like the sensible thing to do.''

She glanced up just in time to see Tracie's smile turn to laughter. ''Oh, Hannah, I wouldn't call marrying Jess sensible. I'd call it taking on a hell of an adventure. But I'm glad that you did. The man needed to be reminded that there's more to life than just being a father to Daniel.''

"But he married me only because of Daniel," Hannah reminded the other woman.

Tracie laughed knowingly. "Well, I wouldn't let that bother you. Jess adores Daniel. That child is his whole life. He wouldn't let just any woman be the boy's mother."

Yes. That much she knew to be true, Hannah thought. And wasn't that one of the greatest honors a man could bestow upon a woman, to ask her to be a mother to his child?

"And Hannah," Tracie went on, breaking into Hannah's musings. "Take my word for it, you're far from plain."

Suddenly, Hannah was laughing and it felt good. "Tracie, you're the funniest person I've ever met."

Tracie laughed along with her. "You'll have to tell Dwight that. He thinks my sense of humor is weird."

After that, the two women finished their coffee and Daniel showed up announcing that he and Oscar were both hungry.

When Hannah explained that there were no groceries and she had no way to get to the store, Tracie was instantly on her feet.

"Well, gosh. I just love an excuse to go shopping. Let's go!"

Hannah was reading a story to Daniel when Jess came home later that day. The minute he walked through the door, Daniel bolted from the couch and rushed to his father's outstretched arms.

As she watched Jess swing the boy up in the air and kiss his cheek, she wondered what it would be like to be greeted with such affection, to know that there was someone who loved her, really loved her, the way Jess loved his son.

"We've been having a good time, Daddy," Daniel said in a rush. "Tracie took us to the store and Hannah bought lots of good things to eat. And she let me have chocolate milk for lunch because I ate all my tuna. And she pushed me on the swing, too!"

"Sounds like you've been having all sorts of fun, son." He put Daniel down on the floor, then looked at Hannah. "Things been going okay?"

She'd almost forgotten how unsettling it was to have his green eyes gliding over her. She cleared her throat and shifted her crossed legs.

"Fine. Are you hungry?" As soon as she spoke the question, she got to her feet and started toward the kitchen.

"No. But I'll take a cup of coffee if you have some made."

He followed her into the kitchen with Daniel racing ahead of the two adults.

"So you met Tracie?" he asked.

Hannah looked up from pouring the coffee to see Jess unbuttoning his shirt. The sight stirred her, but then so did the tiredness in his face.

"Yes. She came over early this morning."

A wry smile touched his mouth. "Knowing Tracie, I'm sure she was dying to meet you."

Jess took the coffee from her and sat down at the table. "She took you to the grocery store?"

Hannah nodded. "She's very nice. I like her."

He arched an eyebrow. "I didn't think she'd be your type."

Hannah didn't know why, but she suddenly had the urge to scream at him. To tell him that on the inside she was a woman just like Tracie, not just a meek little mouse.

"And what is my type, Jess?"

The bite to her voice surprised Jess, making both his eyebrows shoot up. She looked almost angry but for the life of him, he didn't know why. "She's such a chatterbox and she—" He broke off again, unsure of the right thing to say. "Forget it. I'm just glad you like her. Dwight is my best friend, so we'll be seeing him and Tracie from time to time."

Hannah turned away from him and began to wipe the already clean cabinet counter. Behind her, Daniel climbed up in his father's lap.

"Did you chase bad guys today, Daddy?" he asked.

Hannah could hear Jess let out a weary sigh and something about the sound made her ashamed she'd spoken to him in such a waspish tone.

"No. We looked for a long time, but we couldn't find them," Jess told his son.

"Will you come outside and play with me and Hannah? She's gonna show me how to build a castle in the sand."

"No, I think I'd better sleep a little while, sport," Jess said. "Then after I wake up, we'll do something special. Maybe go look for a car for you and Hannah to go places in. How would that be?"

Hannah could hear a smacking kiss, then Daniel's little feet hitting the linoleum. She glanced around to see the boy speeding out the back door. Jess, on the other hand, was wiping a tired hand over his face.

"You don't have to get a car, you know," Hannah felt compelled to say. "I have an old one at home. I should have thought to bring it with me. But since I didn't, I could catch a bus to Lordsburg, then drive it down here."

He frowned at the very idea of her out on the highway alone. And to think of her ever going back to Lordsburg was even worse. For some odd reason, he was afraid if she ever left here, she'd never come back.

Pushing himself to his feet, he reached to unbuckle the holster from around his hips. "You're not going to catch a bus anywhere. I'm going to buy you a car. It's something you'll have to have while I'm working."

"But it's such an expense," she countered. "It would save a lot of money if I went after the one I left in Lordsburg."

He dropped the holstered pistol onto the tabletop, then yanked the tails of his shirt out of his pants. "I don't want you going back to that damn place, hear me?"

Hannah watched, her heart pounding foolishly as he slipped off the shirt and added it to the pile of gunmetal and worn leather.

"Why?"

He looked up at her, his expression grim. "Because I said so. It was no good for me there and it was no good for you. I don't want you going there—unless I'm with you."

Hannah's expression said she clearly didn't understand him. But she wasn't alone. Jess didn't quite understand himself. He only knew that he didn't want her to go anywhere, do anything that might make her want to leave him. The way his mother had left. And Michelle, dear God, he couldn't forget that.

"I was only trying to help," she said in a husky voice, then turned her back to him.

Groaning with frustration, Jess went over to where she was standing. "I know, Hannah."

She didn't turn to him or make any sort of reply. Jess's eyes slid over the back of her red hair, then down to her slim waist. She was wearing a flowered shirt that was faded to a dull yellow. The sight of her in it, standing there with her shoulders squared with a quiet sort of dignity, made

him feel like a bastard. "But I think you need to understand something right now."

Hannah spun around, then gasped as his big hands took
hold of her shoulders.

"What—" She moistened her lips, then tentatively lifted
her eyes to his. "What are you saying?"

Jess's eyes scanned her face, then finally settled on her
mouth. Which was a big mistake because suddenly all he
could think about was kissing her again, the way he'd
kissed her the night she'd accepted his proposal.

"Jess?"

Her voice faded as a rush of blood roared in his ears.
Before he could stop himself, he pulled her into his arms
and lowered his mouth over hers.

Hannah was so shocked by the feel of his mouth on hers
that at first she went stock-still. Even her heart seemed to
forget to beat until the slow, hot exploration of his lips sent
a rush of heat pouring through her body, sizzling every
nerve to a burning awareness.

She moaned and her lips parted. Jess's tongue slipped
inside. The intimate invasion was nothing like Hannah had
ever experienced. Her head reeling, she clung to his bare
shoulders and savored the smell and taste of him, the feel
of his warm skin beneath her fingers, the raw need in his
kiss.

Another minute passed, then two. Finally, his chest
heaving, Jess tore his mouth from hers.

Hannah sucked in long, desperate breaths, then forced
her eyes to open.

To her surprise, he looked as addled as she felt, and her
heart continued its fierce pounding as she asked herself
what it all meant. What was happening to him? To her?

Slowly, she dropped her hands from his shoulders, but her eyes held on to his face as she searched his features for some kind of answer.

"Jess, what—"

"Just remember that I'm your husband, Hannah," he said hoarsely. "And if I want to buy you a damn car, I will."

With that, he grabbed his things from the table and headed out of the kitchen.

Her knees shaking, her mouth burning, Hannah stared at the empty doorway and wondered what would happen if she went after him.

Chapter Eight

"So, you and Hannah have been married for nearly two weeks now. How's marriage agreeing with you?"

Jess looked over at Dwight, who was wrenching the steering wheel back and forth as the pickup bounced and swayed over the deeply rutted road. The blond-headed young man had been Jess's partner for nearly five years and a good friend for just as long. Tonight, they were traveling a rough back road that ran adjacent to the Arizona-Mexico line. It was one of the trails most frequently used by illegals. But so far tonight, they'd seen nothing but sage, cactus and a few mule deer.

"Hannah and I are just fine."

"Hmm. I'm glad to hear it, 'cause you sure haven't looked happy today. In fact, you haven't looked very happy all week."

The truck dived over a short ledge of rock, then settled back onto the desert floor with a bone-jarring thud.

Propping his elbow back out the window, Jess mumbled, "You're imagining things."

Dwight grunted. "How could I? Tracie says I have no imagination."

"Then maybe you should order one of those sex manuals."

"I don't mean that sort of imagination! But maybe you should order one to remind you what it's all about."

Jess snorted. The last thing he needed was to be reminded about sex. It was all he could do to get his mind off the subject for five minutes at a time.

Not bothering to hide his annoyance, he said, "Daniel is a perfect reminder of what it's all about."

Dwight shook his head in disapproval. "Damn it, man. I don't know why you can't forget about Michelle."

"I forgot about Michelle the minute she left town. But I think it would be pretty damn stupid to forget what she's done to me—and Daniel."

The road finally leveled out. Dwight brought the four-wheel drive to a stop and cut the engine.

"From what I've seen of her, Hannah is nothing like Michelle. She isn't going to stick you with a kid, then run out on you."

Jess's laugh was anything but humorous. "You bet she won't, 'cause there's no way in hell I'll ever let it get to that point."

Dwight reached for a paper cup, then filled it with water from a thermos. "Are you sure that's the right way to go about this marriage?"

Jess shot him a scorching glare, but Dwight ignored it.

"I realize Hannah is a little shy," the other man said, "but she's not unattractive by any means. If you'd give it a chance, you two might really hit it off."

Yeah, like they'd hit it off last week in the kitchen, Jess thought wearily. One more minute and he would have been tearing at her dress, forgetting everything he'd learned about women and what they could do to a man's sanity. No! No way was he going to repeat that mistake.

Still, he couldn't deny that the memory of that kiss was still eating at him. He'd tried to forget it, but so far, everything about those few reckless moments was still as fresh in his mind as the night it had happened. Now, all he had to do was look at Hannah and a fire began to smolder inside him.

"We get along just fine the way we are."

Dwight poured out more water and handed it to Jess. "So how does she like her new car?"

Jess shrugged as he swallowed the ice water. "I don't know. She rarely gets in the thing. She's not a goer."

"From what Tracie says, Hannah doesn't think you much like her to go anywhere."

Jess frowned in complete surprise. "That's ridiculous. I don't care where Hannah goes. Within reason," he added as Dwight's eyebrows lifted quizzically.

"Well, she told Tracie that she and Daniel came back from the library the other evening and found you all riled up."

Jess cursed. "I wasn't riled up. I was worried."

"Oh, well. Now, that's different," Dwight said with a knowing grin on his face.

Jess gritted his teeth. "Dwight, I'm warning you—"

The radio on the dashboard crackled with static. Jess turned a knob to squelch the noise.

"—woman with two children a mile east of old highway road," a voice said, finally coming through clearly. "Anyone in the vicinity?"

Jess picked up the mike and informed the dispatcher they were on their way.

Dwight started the engine. "Looks like we gotta get out of here."

"Yeah," Jess said with a heavy sigh. "I just hate it when there's kids. Really hate it."

Hannah laid the brush aside, then peered at herself in the dresser mirror. For years, she'd brushed her long hair before going to bed. To keep it shiny, her mother had instructed her.

Frowning, she slid her hands along the two red curtains of hair framing her face. Maybe it was shiny, she acknowledged as she critically eyed her image. But what difference did it really make?

Actually, these past couple of weeks, Hannah had been wondering a lot about herself. Being married to Jess had done something to her. She was seeing all sorts of things from a different perspective. She'd begun to question herself. About her past and her future.

She'd spent most of her life trying very hard not to be like her mother. She'd played down every aspect of her looks, thinking that if a man should ever look at her, he'd be a good man who would love her. A playboy would never bother with a plain woman, she'd always believed.

But Ted proved that theory wrong fifteen years ago, she thought as she picked up the brush and yanked it through the back of her hair.

Ted Scott. She could barely remember his last name and his face was just a murky memory now. She'd been eighteen and a freshman at college in Deming. It was the first time she'd been away from home and Ted had been the only boy to show her any sort of serious attention. She'd been so naive, so hungry for affection and companionship that she hadn't been able to see that all he wanted was sex. Even after she'd given in to him, she'd still believed he loved her. It wasn't until several days after she'd slept with him and he hadn't come around that the truth began to sink in. She could still remember the humiliation she'd felt when she knocked on his dorm-room door and he'd slammed it shut in her face. Hannah had given her virginity to someone who'd merely considered her a piece of flesh, nothing more.

A few days later, she'd gotten the call that her mother had been injured in a car accident. For a long time afterward, Hannah had carried around a deep-seated guilt. She'd thought that her immoral behavior with Ted had somehow been the reason her mother had been hurt.

Placing the hairbrush on the dresser, Hannah tilted her head, first one way and then the other. She'd matured a lot since then. She no longer felt guilty or believed the accident had happened simply to punish her. And now that she'd married Jess, she was beginning to see that hiding behind a dowdy appearance wouldn't necessarily keep a woman's heart safe. No, as each day passed, she could feel a little more of herself binding to him.

"Hannah? Where are you? We need to talk."

At the sound of Jess's loud voice, Hannah jumped from the dressing table. What in the world was the matter with him? He was going to wake Daniel!

"Hannah?" he blared, closer now.

Hannah glanced desperately around for her robe. When she failed to see it, she rushed out of the bedroom, anyway. It would be better to let him see her in her nightgown than to have Daniel's sleep interrupted.

"I'm here, Jess," she called in a shushed tone as she hurried down the hall and into the living room.

Heading toward the kitchen, Jess turned at the sound of her voice. "I wanted—" He stopped suddenly, the rest of his words lodged in his throat. All she was wearing was a long pink nightgown. Her flaming red hair floated around her shoulders like a shiny cape. He didn't know if she'd been in bed or not, but either way he knew he'd damn sure like to take her there. He'd hate himself in the morning. But could that be any worse than the ache he felt building inside him?

Damn right it could be worse, he snapped at himself. A hell of a lot worse.

Clearing his throat, he purposely fixed his eyes on her face.

"You wanted something?" she said, her voice breathless from rushing down the hallway.

Feeling an extra need for oxygen, himself, Jess drew in a long breath. "Yeah. I wanted to tell you that I don't mind if you and Daniel go places. You can go where you like. Just leave me a note when you do. Okay?"

Not really understanding why he'd considered that so urgent, she said nothing, merely nodded.

"I don't want you thinking I'm possessive, or selfish."

She shook her head, implying that she'd never thought such a thing.

His eyes holding on to her gray ones, he took a couple of steps toward her. "I want you to be happy."

She nodded again as her eyes slowly searched his features. There was a strange look of anguish on his face, a look that she couldn't understand.

"Jess, is something wrong?"

Her soft voice was filled with concern. It was as though she really cared about him, not just about his physical needs, but cared about what he was feeling inside. No woman had ever been that way with Jess Malone.

"No," he said, his voice rough with unguarded emotion. "I'm just—"

Suddenly, he was groaning, reaching for her and pulling her close against him. "I'm just glad you're here," he said against the top of her head.

Hannah didn't understand his strange mood. Nor was she going to question it. She simply closed her eyes and pressed her face against his chest. He smelled like sand and sage and Jess. Her Jess. Her husband.

His hands roamed her back, felt the warmth of her flesh through the thin cotton and instinctively pressed her closer. He knew it was a mistake to hold her like this. But there was an awful emptiness inside him, one that he didn't even know was there until he'd married Hannah. And being with her, holding her close to his heart seemed to be the only way he could fill it up.

"I'm glad I'm here, too," she said, the quiver in her voice muffled by his khaki shirt.

He lifted her face to his. "Are you? Are you, really?"

Hannah began to tremble as she gazed into his green eyes. He was looking at her as if she were precious to him. How could that be? He'd only married her to give Daniel a mother.

"Yes. I am. You—you're very good to me."

How could she say that, much less think it? The only thing Jess had ever tried to be good at was being a father, and there were plenty of times he doubted himself in that department.

Slowly, reluctantly, he set her away from him, before the urge to make love to her overtook his common sense.

"I guess you think I must be losing my mind," he mumbled, turning away from her and rubbing his hand wearily across the back of his neck.

Actually, she didn't know what to think about him, or
the overwhelming need she felt to reach out and touch him,
to have his arms around her again.

Swallowing, she nervously ran her hands down the sides
of her hips. It was a little too late to be embarrassed about
standing here in her nightgown, she told herself, but she
was, anyway.

"No. I just think you look tired. Did something happen at work?"

He glanced over his shoulder at her, wondering how she
was always able to pick up on his moods so quickly.
They'd only been married two weeks. Was he that trans-
parent? If he was, then she could tell that right now he
wanted more than anything to kiss her, hold her, touch her
in ways that he doubted any man had ever touched her.

With a shake of his head, he moved across the room and
sank down onto the couch. There was a floor lamp burning at one end, and as he bent to tug off his cowboy boots,
Hannah watched the pool of light glint in the dark waves
of his hair.

"Nothing happened that doesn't usually happen," he
said tiredly.

He set the dusty boots to one side, then leaned his head
against the couch cushions. Hannah stood watching him,
trying to decide what to do. Did he want to talk? Or eat?
Or did he simply want to be alone?

"Well, that's not entirely true," he said suddenly.
"Something did happen that... bothered the hell out of
me."

Her face full of concern, Hannah took a seat on the
couch at a distance from him. "Were you shot at?"

She hadn't tuned in to the news tonight. Maybe he'd
been involved in a drug raid, or something equally dan-

gerous had taken place. The whole idea made her mouth go dry with fear.

Jess let out a derisive snort. "I wish to God that's all it had been. I'd have rather seen a bullet whizzing by my head than what I saw tonight."

"Someone was dead, or dying?" she ventured.

He shook his head. "No. At least, I hope not. Dwight and I found a young woman out in the desert on an old dirt back road. She was carrying a baby, a girl about four months old and leading a boy of about three. He wasn't even as big as Daniel. She said they'd walked for about six or seven miles."

"Seven miles!" Hannah gasped. "But why? What was she doing out there?"

"My Spanish is far from perfect, but from what I could understand, she was running from an abusive husband."

Hannah's hand unconsciously lifted to her mouth. "How terrible," she whispered. "But why was she out in the desert? Surely there's a shelter in Douglas for women who need it."

Jess grimaced. "Not for women like her. She was an illegal. Living south of Agua Prieta. She slipped over the border with intentions of heading to New Mexico, then farther north before her husband, or we, could catch her."

Hannah supposed the "we" meant the border patrol. Still, the way he'd said it made it sound as if he weren't any better than her abusive husband.

"So what happened? What did you do with her and the children?"

He rubbed his hands over his face, then looked at her. "The only thing we could do. We took her in. It will be up to the Mexican government to see that she gets help."

Aching to touch him, comfort him in some way, Hannah leaned toward him. "Then you shouldn't feel badly,

Jess. You have to do your job. Besides, anything could have happened to them in the desert."

He let out a heavy breath. "Yeah, you're right. But it was hard, Hannah, seeing the desperate, frightened look on her face. The baby was dehydrated from being out in the heat for so long and the little boy's back was blistered raw because he didn't have a shirt. All I could think about was you and Daniel. How grateful I was to know that when I came home, you'd both be here, safe and sound."

A hot, achy lump filled Hannah's throat. Before she lost her nerve, she leaned even closer to him and laid her palm against his cheek.

"No one has ever said anything like that to me before," she whispered, her voice choked with unshed tears. "No one."

The feel of her hand against his face, the soft, yearning look in her gray eyes melted something deep inside Jess. Like a starved man, he blindly reached for her.

"Hannah, sweet Hannah," he said softly, his hands coming up to frame her face.

Knowing if she didn't do something, she was going to wind up in his arms, she said, "You don't want to kiss me, Jess. Back in Lordsburg, you said that wasn't a part of our marriage deal."

Back in Lordsburg, he'd said a lot of things. But the way he felt right now, he couldn't remember any of them, or why he'd said them at all.

"To hell with what I said," he muttered, then gently passed his thumbs over the soft pink flush staining her cheekbones. "Or don't you want me to kiss you?"

Did he have to ask? Couldn't he look at her and tell that all she'd ever wanted from him was his love? Her heart began to pound, making her hands shake so badly that she gripped the front of his shirt in an effort to still them.

"No. Yes. Jess, I—I—"

He stopped her stuttering with his mouth as his hands lowered her down onto the cushions.

Hannah couldn't resist him, even though a little voice inside her head was telling her to. He didn't really want *her*. He merely wanted a woman. She knew that in a few minutes when he came to his senses, he would regret ever having touched her, in the first place. Just like last week in the kitchen when he'd walked out, leaving her heart breaking and her body aching. Still, she couldn't push him away or refuse the thrust of his tongue as he parted her teeth.

To have Hannah's body stretched out beneath him inflamed Jess's senses, made him forget his hellish vow of celibacy. The soft globes of her breasts, the mound of her womanhood pushed against him, tormented his body with promises of ecstasy.

As Hannah wound her arms around his neck, touched her tongue to his, she decided she was crazy. There was no other explanation for this and the things she was feeling. For years, she'd made sure that no man had gotten close enough to touch her. She hadn't wanted a man to touch her. Until Jess. Did that mean she was crazy? Or just in love?

"Hannah, dear God, let me touch you. Let me love you," he whispered hoarsely, his lips pressing a hot trail down her throat.

He didn't want to love her, did he? The question barely had time to fly through her mind before his hands were tugging her nightgown up over her legs and higher still until her bare breasts were exposed to his hungry gaze.

Moaning, Hannah closed her eyes, then gasped aloud as his mouth was suddenly tugging at her nipple, sending hot ripples of excitement shooting through her body.

"This isn't wrong, Jess," she groaned thickly. "Tell me it isn't wrong."

There was a thread of fear in her voice that brought Jess to his senses quicker than if a bucket of cold water had been dashed over his head. Because that fear he heard in her voice echoed the feeling he got every time he thought of her leaving.

Slowly, as if something in him had suddenly died, he pulled her nightgown down over her legs, then got to his feet.

Dazed and trembling, Hannah stared at his back. "Jess?"

"I can't tell you anything, Hannah. I don't know what's wrong or right anymore," he said in a voice rough with emotion.

The slender thread holding her emotions together suddenly snapped. Before she realized what she was doing, she pushed herself off the couch and went to stand in front of him.

"Then maybe you'd better figure it out," she said.

The torment on his face was swiftly replaced with a look of utter surprise. Not only was her voice full of fire, her gray eyes were virtually spitting sparks at him.

"Hannah, I know you're thinking I've gone back on my word. But—"

She shook back the tangle of red hair that had fallen onto her face. "If you think I'm upset about that then—well, you know a lot less about women than I thought you did!"

His eyes widened at her suggestion. "What does that mean?"

Her cheeks were suddenly crimson, but whether it was from anger or embarrassment, Jess wasn't sure. This was a Hannah he'd never seen before.

"What you said or didn't say in Lordsburg doesn't matter. It's the way you're treating me now that I want to know about."

His nostrils flared as he drew in a deep breath. "I'm sorry—" He halted abruptly as she covered her eyes with fisted hands and groaned with frustration.

"I don't want you to be sorry, Jess! I just can't understand any of this. What is it about me that you find so repulsive? My hair? My clothes? My body? Or is it just me, in general?"

She dropped her hands and Jess's heart contracted at the pain he saw in her eyes.

"Hannah, I don't find you repulsive!" Wanting to comfort her, he moved closer, but managed to stop himself from reaching for her shoulders. He was afraid to touch her, he realized. Afraid that this time he might not be able to let her go.

"How could you think that after what happened a few moments ago?"

She looked at him in angry disbelief. "How could I not think it? How do you think it makes me feel when—when you come home and touch me like you really want to, like you mean it and then—" She broke off as tears began to clog her throat.

"Damn it, Hannah, I do touch you because I want to. I want you too much. That's the problem. But I don't understand what you want from me or why you're so angry."

She blinked rapidly as tears scalded the back of her eyes. How could she expect him to understand the way she felt? she asked herself dismally. He didn't really know her. To him, she was just the woman who looked after his son.

"I'm angry because I don't like being used. I don't like being treated like a toy that you can pick up and play with whenever the urge strikes you, or toss aside when you're bored.''

Lifting his eyes to the ceiling, Jess stabbed both hands into his hair and raked his fingers against his scalp. ''You don't know how it is—''

''I know a lot more than you think I do, Jess Malone! I was used by a man once before in my life. I won't ever let that happen to me again.''

His head jerked around to hers. ''What man?''

The astonishment on his face made her even angrier. ''Oh, yes, Jess, I know what it's like to put your trust and your heart in someone else's hands and have it thrown in your face. So, until you decide you really want to make love to me, I don't want you to touch me at all!''

Stunned, Jess's mouth dropped open. But before he could utter a word, Hannah turned on her heel and ran out of the room.

Jess wanted to go after her. He wanted to yell at her that sex had never been a part of the deal and it never would be.

But he couldn't do it. Because it suddenly dawned on him that Hannah hadn't been talking about sex, she'd been talking about making love. And that was something altogether different.

Dazed, he walked over to the couch, sank onto the edge of the cushion and scrubbed his face with both hands. *Until you decide you want to make love, don't touch me at all.*

Well, Hannah, you won't have to worry about my touching you again, he angrily told himself. Because it would be a cold day in hell before he made love to a woman. In fact, hell would have to be freezing over!

Chapter Nine

The next morning, Hannah ventured down to the kitchen and found a note for her on the refrigerator.

> Hannah:
>   I had to leave a little early this morning. Call Tracie and ask her about the ball game tonight. I expect you and Daniel will want to come. See you there.
>
>   Jess

Hannah carefully read every line, then tossed the ragged scrap of paper into the trash. He hadn't said anything about a ball game last night. But then, they hadn't really discussed much, she thought. At least not after that episode on the couch!

Dear God, what he must be thinking of her this morning. Maybe it was for the best that he'd had to leave for work before she'd gotten out of bed. At least she wouldn't have to face him for a few more hours.

"Can I have alphabets this morning?" Daniel asked as he climbed into a chair.

Hannah did her best to shake away thoughts of Jess. "I suppose so. If you'll drink a big glass of orange juice to go with them."

She prepared the cereal and milk for Daniel and made toast for herself. While the two of them ate, she said, "Your daddy left a note and said we were to go to a ball game tonight. Do you know what he's talking about?"

Daniel's face brightened and he nodded vigorously. "Yeah! Daddy plays ball. Him and Dwight."

"What kind of ball?"

Daniel's head cocked to one side as he gave her a look as if to say he thought she was definitely a little slow. "Baseball. My daddy catches the ball. And he can hit it really, really hard. He says when I get just a little bit bigger, I can play, too."

Hannah smiled at the child while her heart melted at his little green eyes. In a few years, he'd look just like Jess. Would she still be around then? Or was Jess going to decide he, or Daniel, didn't need her in their lives?

She was still considering that scary question when the telephone rang. Taking her coffee cup with her, she went to answer it.

"Hannah, it's Tracie. Did I wake you?"

Hannah smiled at the sound of Tracie's voice. They were becoming fast friends and Hannah was beginning to feel very comfortable with her.

"No. Daniel and I were just finishing breakfast. In fact, Jess had to leave early this morning. He left a note saying I should call you about a ball game."

"Oh, yeah. Tonight, they're playing the Blue Hornets."

"Where is the game? Do you usually go?"

"Always. Dwight would think I was terrible if I wasn't in the bleachers cheering them on. Our guys are the Sand Devils. Jess hasn't told you about the league he belongs to?"

Hannah sighed inwardly. He hadn't told her about much of anything unless it was something to do with Daniel's care. Almost all their conversations since they'd been married had been centered on the child, up until last night, when Jess had opened up and talked to her about his job.

For those few minutes, she'd felt almost like a real wife. And when he'd taken her into his arms, whispered against her hair, she'd felt needed, even wanted. Until he'd pushed away from her as though his touching her would put an evil spell on him.

"Hannah? Are you still there?"

"Uh . . . yes. I'm here. And no, Jess hadn't told me. But it seems he expects me and Daniel to be there. So maybe I'd better get directions from you on how to get to the ballpark."

"I'll tell you at the mall. That's why I'm calling. I thought we might go clothes shopping this morning."

"Oh, I don't know, Tracie. I have enough clothes to last for a while and I wouldn't want Jess to think I was being frivolous."

Tracie laughed. "You—frivolous? Hannah, don't be ridiculous. Besides, you're his wife. He's supposed to buy you things."

"I don't know about that," she hedged.

"Well, if you don't want to come for yourself, then you can come for me. I want to pick out some maternity things."

Hannah gasped. "Maternity—are you pregnant?"

"Yes! Yes! Isn't it wonderful? I just found out yesterday."

"Congratulations," Hannah said, meaning it from the deepest part of her heart. She knew Tracie would be a wonderful mother, and from the few times she'd seen Dwight, she figured he would be a good father. The couple deserved to have a child of their own. Still, a tiny pang of regret wound its way around Hannah's heart. She'd never go through the experience of pregnancy or giving birth. She'd never feel the child of the man she loved kicking inside her. But she had Daniel. Jess had given her a son just by signing his name to a piece of paper. So why did she suddenly have the urge to cry?

"I'm very happy for you and Dwight. But Tracie, you're not ready for maternity clothes, are you?"

Tracie laughed. "No! But I can't wait to choose some, anyway. Come on. Say you'll go. It'll be much more fun if you're with me. We'll have lunch."

Maybe it would do her good to get out, Hannah decided, rather than stay home and dwell on Jess. Besides, Daniel loved to go anywhere and he was due a treat. "Okay. We'll come. What time do you want to go?"

"I'll be there in fifteen minutes," Tracie said.

Before the morning was over, Tracie had dragged Hannah through every store and boutique that had anything remotely resembling maternity clothes. She even got excited in the toy store, where Daniel took his time choosing between a yellow dump truck and an orange road grater.

"Just think," she squeaked happily, "it won't be that long before I'll be bringing my own little boy or girl in here."

"Yes, you will," Hannah said, trying her best to smile and share in the other woman's happiness.

Still, Tracie must have picked up on Hannah's melancholy mood, because as they sat waiting on their lunch, she said, "Is something wrong, Hannah? Am I boring you with all this baby talk?"

Hannah quickly shook her head. "Oh, no. You're not boring me at all. I guess I'm just wondering what it must be like for you. To know that you and your husband's child is growing inside you."

Instinctively, she glanced over at Daniel who was making motor noises for the road grater Hannah had purchased for him earlier. She thanked God for the little boy. He'd shown her more love these past two weeks than she'd seen in her whole life.

"Would you like to have a child, Hannah? A sibling for Daniel?"

Tracie's question startled Hannah out of her silent reverie. She looked over at her newfound friend.

"What makes you ask that?"

Tracie shrugged. "I don't know. Maybe it's the way you look at Daniel."

Hannah moved her eyes away from Tracie and glanced across the small eating place filled with noonday regulars. "I love Daniel," she said, then as if to reassure herself that she really did have a son now, she reached over and brushed his bangs off his forehead.

He grinned up at her, then returned his attention to the grater and a pair of flexible toy workmen.

"I know that you love Daniel," Tracie said. "That's why I'm wondering if you'd like another child."

Hannah let out an impatient sigh. "Tracie, I don't know why you're bringing up such a question. You know the situation between Jess and me."

Tracie frowned. "It might not always be that way between the two of you. Especially if you don't want it to be."

Hannah's eyes jerked over to see a calculating smile on Tracie's face. "What do you mean?"

"It means that if you want your marriage to Jess to be a real one, then you've got to do something about it. You've got to make him notice you."

"Notice me?"

Tracie giggled and Hannah could only imagine what was going round in the bubbly blonde's head.

"Yes . . . you know, notice you as a woman."

"He knows I'm a woman, Tracie," Hannah said dully.

Tracie waved her hand airily. "Of course he does. In the general sense. But you need to shake him up. And believe me," she added with a laugh, "Jess Malone has needed to be shaken up for a long time."

Hannah stared at her. "I've heard that when women get pregnant, the sudden surge of hormones often makes them irrational. I'm beginning to think it's happening to you, Tracie."

Tracie crowed with laughter. "I knew you had a sense of humor in you somewhere. And a lot of other things, if you'll just let them come out." Her expression sobered. "Hannah, can I ask you something? Seriously, without your getting offended?"

Even if she'd wanted to, Hannah doubted she could have stopped the woman from asking. "No. I won't be offended. Go ahead."

At that moment, the waitress arrived with their burgers and shakes. Tracie didn't say anything until the woman had left and Hannah was helping Daniel get his meal situated.

"Since the first time I met you, I've wondered why you dress the way you do. And I don't mean that you look bad," she added quickly. "You just look, well—sedate. If you were in your seventies, I could sort of understand it. But you're young and beautiful."

Hannah's hand flew to her knot of hair, then to her heated cheeks. "I'm not anything close to beautiful."

"That's not true," Tracie countered. "I think it's just what you want to believe of yourself."

Hannah grabbed her milk shake and took a long drink. "I'm not—I don't like to be noticed, Tracie. And as for Jess—"

"Why don't you want to be noticed? I thought every woman wanted to be beautiful. I certainly do."

Hannah picked up her burger, but that was as close as she got to taking a bite. "My mother *was* a beautiful woman," she said softly, "but it never got her anything but heartache. I don't want to be like her."

Tracie frowned. "I don't understand. You don't get along with your mother?"

"Oh, yes. I loved her very much."

"Loved?"

Hannah nodded. "She died a little over a year ago. She'd been an invalid for many years and needed my care."

"I'm sorry about that," she said gently. "But I still don't understand."

Hannah's lips twisted ruefully. "For years, my mother worked as a cocktail waitress. That's where she met my father, or so she maintained. I won't ever know that for sure," she said with a sigh. "Anyway, he lived with her a little while, but never married her. After I came along, he left for good. People in Lordsburg gossiped about Rita, my mother, for years, said she supported herself and me by—well, being a lady of the evening."

Tracie's expression was full of compassion. "Was she...a lady of the evening?" Tracie gently urged.

Shrugging, Hannah forced herself to take a bite of her burger. "I don't know. Sometimes I believed she was." She looked at Daniel who was busily chewing his cheeseburger as he pushed the road grater around the salt-and-pepper shakers. Jess had taken desperate measures to see that his son had a mother and she supposed that Rita had taken her own desperate measures to take care of her daughter.

"Whether she was or wasn't really doesn't matter anymore," Hannah said and knew that she truly meant it. For the first time in her life, she knew she could accept and look beyond the reality of her past. "She was my mother and she loved me and took care of me the only way she knew how."

Tracie gave her an encouraging smile. "If you understand that, then why are you still hiding?"

Why was she still hiding? Hannah asked herself. She wasn't in Lordsburg anymore. No one here was watching her, just waiting to see if the plain old moth would change into a butterfly like her mother, who'd flitted from one man to the next.

"You're right, Tracie. I have been hiding. But I've done it for so long now that I don't know how to quit doing it. I don't even know that I could."

Her face full of excitement, Tracie reached across the table and squeezed Hannah's hands, hamburger and all. "Oh, yes, you can! And I'm going to help you. Are you ready to try?"

"Try what?" Daniel asked, looking up from his toys.

"All sorts of new things," Tracie said to him. "Are you tired? Are you ready to go home yet, Daniel?"

"No. Do we have to? I wanna get ice cream. Can I, Mommy?" he said, turning to Hannah.

Her heart swelled with love. It was the first time he'd actually called her mommy. She hoped he would call her that for the rest of her life.

"You sure can, son. Chocolate with lots of whipped cream."

"Not too much whipped cream, though," Tracie interjected with a laugh. "You've got to save room for a hot dog tonight at the ball game, remember. And once we get there, we're gonna give Jess a big surprise."

"We are?" Daniel asked with childlike innocence. "What kind of surprise?"

Tracie looked over at Hannah and winked. "A good one!"

For the next few hours, Hannah felt as if she'd been transported to another world. The first thing Tracie did was yank her into the nearest styling salon. Hannah had never been to one before. All she'd ever done with her hair was shampoo it, then secure it into a knot or a French braid. When the ends became ragged, she trimmed them herself.

So when the operator ushered her over to a seat, she was a little bit afraid and a whole lot excited. Especially when Tracie said, "Give her the works. Shampoo, haircut, style, makeup and manicure."

"Tracie!" Hannah gasped. "Let's just do a little at a time. Don't you think?"

"Nonsense!" With Daniel in tow, Tracie marched over to where Hannah sat in the pink swivel chair. "You want to do this right." She glanced up at the operator, a young man who looked as if he was itching to dig his hands into Hannah's red hair. "Make her looks stylish, but not overdone. You know what I'm trying to say? Make everything subtle, but effective."

"I know exactly, Mrs. Towson. Just give me an hour and a half and Mrs. Malone will look fabulous."

Later that evening, on their way to the ballpark, Tracie said, "Hannah, you look better than fabulous. You look incredible. I'm downright green with envy." She laughed with anticipation. "As for Jess, I can't wait to get a look at his face when he sees you."

Hannah took a deep breath and tried to still her racing heart. What was Jess going to think? That she'd lost her mind? That she was pathetically trying to be something she could never be?

She glanced down at her lap, still not able to believe those were her legs in a pair of blue jeans. And the peach-colored T-shirt that Tracie had insisted she wear with them was like wearing nothing at all. It left her arms bare and clearly outlined the shape of her breasts. She'd never worn anything so daring, so young and carefree. Had she lost her mind, or just now found it?

"I feel so different." She squared around on the seat to look at Tracie. "And all those clothes I bought. What will I do with the old ones?"

"We're going to pack them up and give them to charity," Tracie said with a measure of gladness. "They'll do some poor woman in the nursing home a lot more good than they were doing you."

"I guess I did look pretty matronly," Hannah said, then felt a rush of doubt flooding through her. "But what if Jess hates my looking this way?"

Tracie made a tsking noise with her tongue. "If he does, then he's more messed up than I thought."

"Where are those women?" Jess voiced the question as he tossed his catcher's mitt onto the dugout floor. "I left

Hannah a note to call Tracie. Do you think something has happened to them? Daniel always likes to see the start of the game. Now they've missed it."

"They'll be here," Dwight said patiently. He took a seat on the bench beside Jess. "Knowing Tracie, she's been out all afternoon, shopping for baby furniture, and has forgotten the time. You know how it is when a woman first learns she's pregnant, they get so excited they don't know what's going on around them."

"No. I don't know," he said sharply.

Michelle had been furious and shouting abortion when she'd discovered she was pregnant with Daniel. It was something Jess never wanted to go through again.

Seeing the grimace on his partner's face, Dwight said, "Sorry, Jess, I guess I'm not thinking too well, either. That wasn't the thing to say to you. But believe me, Michelle was far from the norm."

Jess reached over and gave Dwight an affectionate punch on the shoulder. "It doesn't matter. I'm glad that you and Tracie are finally going to have a child. I mean that."

At the other end of the dugout, a big barrel-chested man with a clipboard in his hand got to his feet. "Okay, Blakemore, you're up to bat. Then Parkenson. Towson, you're third. And Malone, you'll be batting clean up."

For the next few minutes, everyone was watching the first batter for the Sand Devils. That is, everyone except Jess. He was scanning the bleachers for his wife and son.

Had he made her so angry last night that she wouldn't come? Was it presumptuous of him to think she'd even care to watch him play baseball? Why should she, a little voice inside him asked. You didn't even bother telling her you belonged to a league, much less invite her to come to a game. You haven't bothered telling her much of anything, unless it was something to do with Daniel, the house or the car.

Dropping his elbows on his knees, he bent his head and pinched the bridge of his nose. All day long, his thoughts had been on Hannah, alternating between the things she'd said to him last night and the way she'd looked when she'd talked about him touching her as if he meant it. Did she really want him to make love to her?

No, damn it! He wasn't even going to contemplate the question. He'd married her to give Daniel a mother. Not to get himself a sex partner. He had to remember that!

"There they are," Dwight said, then his mouth flopped open and he thumped Jess on the back. "Look . . . at that! Is that Hannah? Your Hannah?"

Jess's head jerked upward to follow Dwight's line of vision. Tracie had already taken a seat on a vacated part of the wooden bleacher. Beside her, Daniel was wiggling into place, and standing up beside him was a woman holding a box of food from the concession stand.

His eyes squinting, Jess leaned forward. Dear God, was that Hannah? The woman was tall like Hannah, slim like Hannah, and her hair was the same color. But that was where the similarity ended. This woman was dressed in blue jeans and a T-shirt. Her red hair was loose and lay in feathery waves around her head and shoulders.

"Jess, is that her?" Dwight asked again.

A strange feeling in the pit of his stomach, Jess fell back against the dugout wall with a soft thump. "Yeah. I think so."

"Boy, talk about a transformation! What did you do to her?"

Jess glared at his partner. "Not one damn thing!"

"Say, Dwight," one of the men farther down the bench called out, "who's the redheaded dish with Tracie? A long-lost sister you haven't told us about?"

"Yeah, Dwight," another man added. "When do we get to meet her? I need a date Friday night and she's just what I've been looking for."

Jess turned a thunderous look on the men, while Dwight coughed and shuffled his feet.

"I don't think Jess would like that much, guys. That's Hannah, his new wife."

The two men's jaws literally fell open.

"Well, damn, Jess, how come you've been hiding her?" one of them asked.

"Yeah, I'd like to know where you found her. I'd go see if there are any more like her left," the younger of the two added.

Jess reached over and picked up a Louisville Slugger. Tapping the end against the dirt floor, he said, "Moffet, it wouldn't do you any good if you looked all over the state of Arizona. No woman worth a grain of salt would have you."

The other man laughed, although it was obviously forced. "Well, I'd sure like to know what you have, Jess, 'cause you always seem to get the pretty ones."

Jess knocked the end of the bat against the toe of his cleat. Oh, yeah, he got the pretty ones, all right. Michelle had been real pretty, so beautiful in fact that just looking at her would make a man's mouth water. But what had pretty gotten him then? What would it get him now?

No, he thought grimly. He didn't want Hannah to be pretty. He just wanted her to be his.

Chapter Ten

Daniel was asleep on a blanket, his head resting on Hannah's thigh. The game had just ended and Dwight and Jess climbed the bleachers to where the two women sat waiting for their husbands.

"Nice to see you again," Dwight said to Hannah.

"Hello, Dwight," Hannah said shyly.

"Tracie," Jess said with a nod to the other woman, but his eyes were glued to his wife. Hannah didn't just look different from far off. Even close up, the sight of her knocked him sideways.

"Jess was beginning to worry when you two were late. Did you have trouble with the car?" Dwight asked Tracie.

Rising to her feet, Tracie slung her arm affectionately around her husband's shoulders. "No," she said with an impish smile. "Hannah and I did a lot of interesting things today and time got away from us."

"Well, we'd better get home," Dwight said, hugging her to his side. "I don't want you overtiring yourself."

Tracie looked at Hannah and gave her a conspiratorial wink. "Call me in the morning, Hannah, and we'll do that charity work we were talking about."

Hannah nodded.

"Oh, by the way, Jess," Tracie called out as she and Dwight started down the bleachers, "you played a great game tonight. I don't think I've ever seen anyone hit the four-hundred-foot fence before. If I didn't know better, I'd have thought you were trying to impress your new wife."

Jess knew the other woman was teasing him, but tonight he wasn't in the mood for Tracie's brand of humor.

"It's just all part of the game," Jess drawled.

Tracie laughed and the couple waved goodbye. Once Tracie and Dwight were down off the bleachers and headed toward the parking lot, Jess whirled on Hannah.

"What has she been doing to you?"

His outburst was so unexpected that Hannah literally gasped out loud. "*She* hasn't been doing anything to me," she said quietly. "Would you mind lifting Daniel for me? I'm afraid my leg has fallen asleep."

Jess wasn't ready to leave just yet. He wanted to have it out with her here and now. He wanted to know what had happened to her, to his Hannah.

But how could he? He couldn't start making demands, telling her how to comb her hair, what sort of clothes she had to wear. Even if they were husband and wife in every sense of the word, he couldn't start acting *that* possessive! But God help him, he wanted to.

The muscles in his face as tight as stretched barbed wire, he reached down and lifted Daniel from his makeshift bed. Deliberately avoiding looking at Jess, Hannah got to her feet and folded the blanket over her arm. Not only was her leg numb, she realized as she followed Jess down the bleachers and out to the pickup, her whole body, even her mind, was numb.

She'd never been through such a day as this before. Her emotions had run the gamut from fear to hope, then surprise and joy. Now she felt nothing but numbing pain.

They didn't speak during the short ride home. Hannah told herself she didn't care about the strained silence. She'd already gotten his reaction and it hadn't been pleasant. So much for her plans to make him take notice.

Perhaps it was as Tracie had said, Jess was more messed up than anyone thought. Maybe there wasn't a woman on this earth who could ever really touch him. She'd certainly been foolish to think she could even try.

Once they returned home, Jess carried Daniel to the child's bedroom. Hannah followed the two and quickly changed the little boy's jeans and shirt for a pair of striped pajamas.

Jess stood at the doorway watching. He'd never been able to change Daniel's clothes without waking him. Yet, as Hannah performed the task, the child remained as limp as a rag right on up until she covered him and switched off the light.

Maybe it was the gentleness of her hands, Jess thought. Or maybe Daniel just unconsciously knew that he had a mother now and could sleep soundly knowing she would be there to take care of him.

"Good night, my sweet boy," Hannah whispered as she leaned over him and kissed his smooth, rosy cheek.

The tender sight stung Jess somewhere deep inside. He'd never had a mother to do that for him. Daniel hadn't, either. Until now. Until Hannah had come into their lives. He couldn't mess things up now, he told himself. He had to be a father first and put this crazy, insatiable craving he had for Hannah out of his mind.

Feeling the desperate need to distance himself from her, Jess headed to the kitchen. If he was lucky, he thought as he opened the refrigerator door, maybe Hannah would go to bed and he wouldn't be tempted to do or say something he would later regret.

"If you're hungry, there's leftover ribs I could heat up for you."

Something about the softness of Hannah's voice melted his insides. Slowly, he shut the refrigerator door and turned to see her standing in the doorway.

She moved into the room, her expression placid, as though his outburst at the baseball field had never happened. Jess felt oddly sick. As if he knew he was about to fall into a pit of flames but there was nothing he could do about it.

"There's also some potato salad left. You probably couldn't have had much to eat with the ball game and all."

Hannah was not a woman to inspire anger in a man. How could she? She was the epitome of gentleness and kindness. From the day she'd walked into the house as his wife, she'd always put him and Daniel first. She saw to their needs before her own. The house was always clean, the laundry always done, delicious meals were always waiting for him.

No. Hannah never gave him a reason to be angry with her. But he was. He was angry as hell, because somehow, some way, she'd made him want her. She'd made him love her. He didn't know when it had happened, or why. But tonight, when his teammates had looked at her, as men had looked at women since the beginning of time, he'd wanted to knock their heads off.

He'd been struck with jealousy. Because those men were seeing Hannah the way he should have seen her from the very start. As a beautiful, desirable woman.

"I'm not hungry," he told her. "A glass of orange juice will do."

"I'll get it for you," she said, swishing past him on the way to the refrigerator.

Jess went to the kitchen table and pulled out a chair. From the corner of her eye, Hannah watched his tall frame sink wearily into the seat. She'd been angry with him earlier at the ballpark. But she wasn't angry now. It was a useless emotion, and besides, it wasn't his fault that he didn't find her appearance to his liking. Face it, Hannah, you can't make a person notice you, or even love you, if they don't want to.

"Did you have a hard day at work?" she asked as she carried the juice over to him.

It was a question asked by millions of spouses every day, yet Jess still wasn't used to hearing it. He'd never expected a woman to be around long enough to care whether he had a bad day or not.

"The immigration laws and poor living conditions across the border make every day a hard day," he said, then thanked her as he took the glass of juice. "Dwight and I were rocked today. Our truck looks like it's been through a hell of a hailstorm."

Wide-eyed, Hannah pulled out a chair beside him and eased onto the edge of it. "Rocked? You mean people actually threw rocks at you?"

He nodded. "Sometimes, when things like that happen, I have to ask myself if this is really the United States, or if I've been transplanted to some Middle Eastern country where war and acts of violence are an everyday occurrence."

"I'm just glad you weren't hurt," she stressed, her eyes traveling over the tired lines of his face.

It would be wonderful, she thought, if she could just reach out and touch his cheek, tell him how much she cared about him. "But why would anyone want to throw rocks at you? Why would they want to harm you?"

He drained off the last of the juice, then combed his fingers through his hair. "Because they think with us border patrolmen out of the way, their problems would be solved. They could go wherever they want, do whatever they want. Others just don't like us because we're the law. We represent authority, something they wish they had."

"So why have you been a border patrolman for so many years?" she asked, glad at least they were back to talking.

He gave her a wan smile. "Somebody's got to do it. And maybe I'm just a glutton for punishment."

"Or maybe you like that authority you were just talking about," she suggested.

Mild surprise crossed his face as he asked himself once again how she always managed to know things about him before he did. "Yeah. You're probably right. I like enforcing right and wrong. I just wish the line between the two didn't get blurred so often."

"Yes. I'm sure that's true," she said, remembering how torn he was over the mother and two children he and Dwight had found in the desert.

A minute, then two passed in silence. Finally, Hannah got to her feet. "Well, I guess I'll go to bed."

She turned away from the table, then instantly felt Jess's hand come around her wrist like a steel band.

Her eyes lifted quizzically to his.

"I—uh, wanted to say something."

Hannah's heart started to pound against her breast. There was an odd light in his eyes, one she'd never seen before, nor understood.

"Yes?" she asked, her throat suddenly so tight, she could barely get the word out.

"Back at the ballpark, I—" He rubbed his hand across his jaw, then swallowed. "Well, I didn't mean to shout at you."

Surprise flickered over her face. "You didn't shout at me."

His gaze blatantly swept over her rich, glossy hair, the subtle makeup on her face. "I just—couldn't believe I was looking at you."

"I'm sorry you don't like the change," she said and meant it. She was sorry for so many reasons.

There was a tight ache in Jess's chest, a strange sort of pain he'd never felt before. Slowly, he got to his feet and looked into her clear gray eyes. "I didn't say that. Hell, Hannah, a man would have to be blind not to see that you're a beautiful woman."

He thought she was beautiful? No. He couldn't. She was plain old Hannah. The same Hannah who'd been shunned for years. There was no reason to think he wouldn't shun her now.

"I'm nowhere near beautiful," she whispered, but his words had thrilled her to the very core of her being.

Awed by the change in his wife, Jess reached up and tunneled his fingers into her thick, glossy hair. She still smelled like lavender, and the scent was somehow reassuring to him.

"What made you do this, Hannah? Did Tracie push you into it?"

Hannah was suddenly quivering from the touch of his fingers, his nearness, the raw look of hunger on his face. Was that look for her?

"No, Jess. It was something I wanted to do for myself."

"But why? Was it something I said? Was it because of last night?"

She laid her hand on his forearm. It was warm and gritty with sand. She loved the hardness of it, the strength beneath her fingers. It was all she could do to keep her hand from sliding up and curving over his shoulder.

"No, it wasn't last night. I guess it was leaving Lordsburg and getting married. I'm living a different life now and—" She stopped midsentence. He was so close! She couldn't think. Couldn't breathe. If she didn't put some space between them, she was going to wind up falling straight into his chest.

She took a step back, then another, until her bottom bumped into the edge of the table.

"And?"

Fixing her eyes on the toe of her sneakers, she took a deep breath and went on, "I was talking to Tracie today about my mother."

"You were?"

She could hear surprise in his voice, but she wasn't brave enough to look up at him. "I told her how she'd always been gossiped about. I even told her why. And I realized then that I didn't have to keep proving to everyone that I wasn't like my mother, that I wasn't a prostitute."

Jess felt something in his heart rip apart. "Oh, Hannah," he said softly.

She looked up at him then, and her eyes begged him to understand. "She wasn't a bad woman, Jess. Not really."

Jess shook his head. "I never thought she was."

A soft smile tilted her lips. "No. You never did. I remember you sometimes carried her grocery bags in for her."

His smile was reflective. "And you were always standing off to one side of the room, pretending that you weren't looking at me. But I knew you were."

"You remember that—about me?"

Everything inside him was being drawn to her and he could no more stop himself from moving closer than he could stop himself from breathing. "I remember a lot of things about you, Hannah. I remember how impressed I was by your high marks in school. And I used to wonder why you didn't like boys. I even wondered what it would be like to kiss you."

The last words were said very softly. In contrast, Hannah's heart began to pound harder and harder. "I can't imagine why. You'd probably already kissed every girl in high school."

One corner of his mouth cocked upward. "Maybe that's why. You were a mystery to me. You were always so serious. I imagined you would probably kiss that way, too."

"Oh, Jess." It was all she could say. She'd never dreamed he'd given her a second thought.

His green eyes holding her gaze, he touched her cheek with the tips of his fingers. "Last night, you said not to touch you unless I meant to make love to you. Well, that's what I want. Now. This very second."

Hannah didn't have time to be shocked. Then, his hands were crushing her to his chest, his mouth devouring hers, telling her that this time was different. This time, he knew exactly what he wanted, and she was the only woman who could give it to him.

Hannah clung to him and kissed him and reveled in the sensations rushing through her. He smelled like dust and sweat and Jess. Her wonderful Jess. And suddenly, she couldn't get close enough to his body. Or his heart.

"Oh, Jess," she breathed when his mouth finally broke from hers. "Are you sure about this?"

"I know I want you," he murmured against her throat. "Like I've never wanted any woman."

Bending, his arm came around the back of her thighs and lifted her. Hannah didn't protest, she instinctively wrapped her arms around his neck and buried her face against his shoulder. She loved Jess. Loved him with every fiber of her being. She didn't want to turn back now.

The hallway was dark, but in the bedroom, slats of moonlight striped his bed. Near the head of it, Oscar was curled into a tight ball. Jess brushed the cat aside, then lay Hannah gently among the pillows.

Lying close beside her, his hands reached to frame her face, then moved into her hair as he brought his lips against hers. Hannah moaned with sheer longing and pressed herself to the length of him.

His hands splayed across her back, slid to her waist, then on down to cup her bottom and draw her hips against his. Even through their jeans, she could feel the bulge of his desire. Just knowing she had that much effect on him fueled the flames that were already licking at her insides.

"Hannah, I've wanted you for so long. Too long. Don't ask me if this is wrong. I don't want to think about that now. I just want to feel you. I just want your arms around me," he whispered hoarsely.

"You're my husband, Jess," she murmured, "and I'm your wife. This is the way it's supposed to be. The way it was meant to be."

Jess didn't know about that. He only knew he could no longer fight the longing inside him.

"I hope you're right, Hannah. Dear God, I hope you're right," he groaned, then quickly tugged the peach-colored T-shirt over her head.

She was wearing a lacy bra that just managed to cover her nipples. The erotic sight of her pale ivory breasts so soft and smooth against the lace sent his senses reeling. Yet he didn't stop to taste the sweetness of her flesh. Instead, he continued removing her jeans and panties and then his own clothes.

Hannah had thought she would be embarrassed to see him naked and even more so for him to see her. Yet tonight, it all felt right and natural. Tonight, she knew she looked beautiful to him and she wanted to give him the joy of seeing her.

As he started to rejoin her on the bed, Hannah reached to unfasten the clasp holding her bra. Jess's hand instantly covered hers, stilling her fingers.

"No. Let me do it," he said, his knuckles brushing against her breast as he unfastened the flimsy straps of fabric. "Let me do everything for you, Hannah."

Her breasts spilled free of the bra and she shuddered as his head bent and his mouth brushed warm and teasingly against her throbbing nipples.

"You're not afraid, are you?" he mouthed against her. "You're not afraid for me to make love to you?"

How could she be afraid of him? Of this? He was taking her to a place she'd never been, but had always longed to go.

Winding her legs around his, she arched against the heat of his body, inviting him to make their union complete.

"I'm not afraid, Jess. I've wanted you for a long time, too. Just like—this!"

She moaned softly as he entered her, but Jess hardly knew if the sound had come from him or her. The feel of her soft heat surrounding him, loving him, was so overwhelming that for a long moment he couldn't move, he simply gazed upon her face as wave after wave of hot, sweet sensations poured over him.

Fearing she had already disappointed him somehow, Hannah gripped his forearms. "Jess? Is something wrong?"

Through the fog of desire, her voice came to him. He lowered his head and pressed his lips against hers. "No, my beautiful wife. Nothing is wrong." He brushed the hair off her forehead, then slowly began to move inside her. "I just want to make this moment last forever."

Chapter Eleven

The next morning, Hannah awoke in Jess's bed and knew before she looked that he was already gone.

Throwing on her robe, she dashed to the kitchen to see if he'd left a note on the refrigerator door.

He had and it read:

Hannah:
    Had to leave early.

                                                                Jess

She plucked the small square of paper out from under the magnet and told herself not to be disappointed. Just because they'd made love didn't mean he would stay home from work.

But he could have said something, anything to let her know that he loved her and that he wanted to spend the day with her. Who said anything about Jess loving you, a little voice inside her head asked. He never said he loved you.

Hannah tossed the note into the wastebasket, then walked to the back door and gazed out at the rising sun. No, he hadn't said anything about loving her. But a man couldn't make the sort of passionate love Jess had made to her and not feel love in his heart.

Oh, yes, he loved her, she thought dreamily. She knew it with everything inside her.

"Mommy, why are you so happy this morning?" Daniel asked a few minutes later as Hannah told him a funny story over breakfast. "Does your oatmeal taste that good?"

Hannah laughed. "My oatmeal is delicious," she said. "And it's in my tummy. Right where yours needs to be." For emphasis, she gave his stomach a little tickle.

Giggling, he pointed to his bowl. "I'm nearly finished. See?"

She looked at his bowl. "Good. Because we have lots to do today."

"What are we going to do, Mommy? Are we going to take Peanuts for a walk to the park?"

Hannah began gathering dirty dishes and plopping them into a sink of sudsy water. But she might as well have been walking on clouds and gathering rosebuds. Jess was really her husband now. He loved her and wanted her. It was like a dream come true and her heart was so full of joy, she could hardly bear it.

"No, we'll take the dog to the park tomorrow. Today, we're going to the grocery store, then we're going to make Daddy something special."

"We are?" Daniel jumped down from his chair and went to stand by Hannah at the sink. "Can I help, too?"

Hannah bent down and gave him a fierce hug. "You sure can, my little darling."

Jess stared blankly out the dusty windshield as the pickup truck rocked along the desert back road. He and Dwight had been driving for miles, searching for a beat-up green van that had supposedly been used to transport illegals into Arizona, then east into New Mexico. So far they hadn't seen a sign of it.

"Tracie is still walking on air," Dwight said as he steered the pickup over the two rough ruts that barely resembled a road. "She's already designing the spare bedroom into a nursery. In a few days, she'll probably have Hannah over there helping her hang paper with clowns or Mother Goose figures on it."

"Hmm."

"Personally, I'd rather the baby stay in our room with us. But Tracie seems to think he'll need his own space. What do you think? Did you let Daniel sleep in your room?"

What was Dwight saying? Something about Daniel? Frowning, he looked across the seat to his friend. "Sorry, I wasn't listening. Did you ask me something?"

Dwight rolled his eyes and sighed impatiently. "Jess, I swear you've been in another world all day. What the hell is the matter with you?"

"Nothing," he muttered, but the tight grimace on his face said he was in sheer torment.

"You know," Dwight began thoughtfully, "if you could ever get past this hang-up you have about women, then you and Hannah could have a child of your own. A brother or sister for Daniel. It would be wonderful for the boy. Wonderful for all three of you."

Jess started to remind Dwight of what Betty had done to him and his father, of what Michelle had done to him and Daniel. But none of that ever got past his lips. Dear God, Hannah could be pregnant now, he realized with a jolt. He hadn't used any precautions last night. As for Hannah, she'd come into this marriage thinking she didn't need protection.

Protection, hell, he snorted to himself. He'd been the one who'd needed protecting. He'd fallen for her like a ton of bricks. Oh, Lord, what had he done? Why had he set himself up to be hurt all over again?

No, he wouldn't just be hurt, he corrected himself. He'd be mangled if this marriage didn't go right. Everything with Hannah was so different than what he'd gone through with Michelle. Now that he looked back on it, he realized that he and Michelle had been little more than bed partners. Sex had been the only thing holding them together.

It wasn't like that with him and Hannah. He loved her. He'd known it even before last night. And now? Well, now that he'd actually made love to her, he felt like a man lost. His heart was no longer his; it was Hannah's. And he was afraid—scared to death.

He had to do something fast. Today! He couldn't let himself become obsessed with love for her—like his father had been with Betty.

"Jess? Have you heard anything I've been saying?"

Dwight's voice called him back to the here and now. His face set with grim determination, Jess looked over at the younger man. "No way, buddy. You can be the romantic fool. You can have the love and the babies and the happily-ever-after. It's not meant for me. Never was. Never will be."

Hannah sat on the couch with the TV off and the lights dimmed. But the moment Jess's headlights swept across the driveway, she rushed to the kitchen and lighted three candles on the carefully set table.

As soon as the little flames were glowing, she ran back to the living room and opened the door just in time for Jess to step over the threshold.

"Oh, Jess," she cried softly, flinging her arms around his neck. "I've missed you so much today." And as proof, she kissed one cheek, his chin, then the opposite cheek.

Stunned by her affectionate greeting, Jess momentarily forgot everything. His face pressed against her hair, his hands found her slender waist and clung.

"Come on, Jess," she said shyly, pulling away from him and taking his hand in hers. "I have something special for you."

She began leading him toward the kitchen, and as they went, he glanced over his shoulder at the darkened living room. "Where's Daniel?"

"He was waiting for you, but about an hour ago he fell asleep. So I put him to bed. He's going to be disappointed in the morning."

In the kitchen, Hannah left him by the door to switch on the light over the cabinets. When it came on, Jess stared at the candlelit table, then at her.

She was wearing a dress the color of jade. It was nipped in at the waist with a wide belt of the same color. There were no sleeves on it and the neck was scooped low. Pinned over one breast was a tiny cat done in rhinestones. Her flaming hair bounced around her face and shoulders, her rosy lips were smiling just for him. She looked so lovely, it very nearly took his breath away and he knew the job he had ahead of him was going to be sheer hell.

"Is this—" he glanced over at the table where the candlelight gently flickered over the dishes and long-stemmed glasses "—is it your birthday?"

She laughed and the sound had him looking back at her. He'd rarely heard her laugh. She hadn't even talked that much since they'd married. Now she was doing both. And she looked so very happy. It radiated from her face, like the glow of moonlight on a smooth, clear lake.

What was he doing, he wondered. Was he crazy for not going to her this very minute and sweeping her up into his arms? His body was certainly begging him to.

"No," she answered, smiling at him. "This is for you. Since we didn't have a wedding dinner, I thought . . . well, I thought we could have a homemade one."

Hannah motioned for him to take a seat at the table. "Go ahead and sit. I've been keeping the food warm. All I have to do is carry it over."

He hung his gun and holster over the back of one of the dining chairs, then took a seat in the one next to it.

Satisfied that he was making himself comfortable, Hannah went after the food. She'd cooked pot roast with potatoes, carrots and baby onions. There were also tiny green peas in cream sauce and yeast rolls.

Once she had it all on the table, she went to the refrigerator and pulled out a bottle of wine. Jess's eyebrows shot up as she handed it to him.

"Do you know how to open it?" She laughed nervously as she took a chair just to his right. "I've never even bought spirits before. And I didn't know what I was doing, so I just told the man I wanted something to go with beef."

Jess knew he shouldn't let things go any further, but all he could seem to do was grip the wine bottle and stare at the beautiful oval of her face.

"You've . . . gone to a lot of trouble," he finally managed to say.

She touched his hand. It was all Jess could do to keep from grabbing handfuls of red curls and tugging her mouth to his. Just thinking of the taste of her, the passion they'd shared last night set a torturous flame afire in the pit of his stomach.

"It wasn't any trouble. I loved every minute of it," she assured him.

He opened the wine and they began to eat. She asked him about his work. He told her about him and Dwight hunting the van. In return, he asked her about Daniel and what his son had been doing all day.

The question had Hannah jumping to her feet and going over to the far end of the kitchen. "Daniel helped me in the kitchen today," she told him, a smile in her voice. "He's quite a little chef."

When she returned to the table, Jess looked up to see she was carrying a white, three-tiered cake decorated with ornamental frosting.

"I thought you said this wasn't your birthday," he said.

"Jess," she scolded playfully, "this is supposed to be a wedding cake. Daniel and I worked on it all afternoon."

She placed it carefully on an empty spot at the end of the table, then cast him an eager glance. "I know it looks a little droopy here and there, but Daniel was having such fun squeezing on the icing, I didn't have the heart to make him stop."

And she seemed so utterly happy that he didn't have the heart to do what he was about to do. But he had to, he fiercely told himself. In the long run, it would be best for everyone.

She started back to her seat. Jess quickly shot to his feet to intercept her. "Uh—Hannah, there's something I want to talk to you about," he said, drawing her away from the table.

She glanced back at their waiting meal. "But we haven't finished eating. Can't we talk over our food?"

Jess shook his head and at that very moment he didn't think he'd ever be able to eat again.

"No. We'll finish later."

He ushered her into the living room and sat her down beside him on the couch. She immediately scooted to the edge of the cushion and squared her knees around to his.

"Is something wrong, Jess? Don't tell me rocks were thrown at you again? It scares me to even think about it."

"No. That didn't happen," he said and she curled her hands around both of his and gave them a gentle squeeze.

"I've got to confess," she said, before he could go on. "I've felt like a giddy idiot all day long. I used to think all that stuff about newlyweds was just nonsense. But now I know it's not. And I don't know what you've done to me, Jess, because I can't quit chattering."

Her voice dropped on the last few words and her expression grew serious. Slowly, she reached out and touched his cheek, the side of his hair and finally the corner of his mouth. "Oh, Jess, you've made me so happy," she whispered, her eyes suddenly brimming with tears. "So happy I could die from it."

Jess didn't move or say a word. He couldn't. He felt as if the life was slowly being snuffed out of him, and he was helpless to do anything to stop it.

Seeing the torment on his face, Hannah said, "Jess, I can see something is wrong. Tell me."

Jess cleared his throat and took a deep breath. "I wanted to talk to you about last night."

He was going to tell her he loved her, she thought. He was going to say he was sorry because he hadn't told her sooner. And she was going to tell him that she loved him, too. That she'd loved him for always, or so it seemed.

"Yes," she urged, her gentle smile encouraging him to go on.

Jess muttered something under his breath and looked away. "I think—I've been thinking about it today and I've decided that—last night was a big mistake."

Hannah reeled back, the force of his words hitting her as surely as a slap across the face. A mistake? The word whirled in her head as though it were a foreign one and she didn't quite understand the meaning. How could he call last night a mistake? It was the most beautiful, wonderful thing that had ever happened to her. For the first time in her life, she'd felt wanted, loved. For the first time, she'd had someone to share her innermost self with. Someone to race to the moon with. That couldn't be a mistake!

"Jess—I—do you really mean that?"

Her throat was suddenly so achy, she had to keep swallowing to get the question out, and as she waited for his answer, her palms filled with ice-cold sweat.

"I do." He looked at her and saw pain and disbelief sweep across her face. In that moment, he hated himself for hurting her, for lacking the courage to give her what she wanted.

"I think it would be better if we forgot last night ever happened and started over again. The way we'd first planned. A sexual relationship between us would just cause problems."

"Problems, for whom?" she wanted to know.

For him, damn it, he wanted to yell. Every time he made love to her, he'd lose a little more of himself to her, and every time, he'd wonder how long it would be before she decided to pack up and leave.

"For both of us," he answered. Then, unable to bear being this close to her, he got to his feet and went to stand by the double windows overlooking the front lawn. "Remember, we agreed this marriage would be platonic. That's the way I want it to be."

"And what about last night? We'll just forget about what happened between us and go back to being a man and a woman sharing the same house and the same son?"

"That's right," he said, relieved that she was speaking in such a calm, rational way.

Hannah wanted to jump to her feet, to scream at him that his deciding had come a little slow. Painfully slow, in fact. But she didn't. Screaming and crying wouldn't change anything. He regretted making love to her. He didn't want to repeat it. And she wasn't going to beg for favors.

"I don't think it would be—" he glanced over his shoulder at her "—very smart of us. Especially since we planned to make this first year of our marriage a trial thing."

Numbly, Hannah rose to her feet.

"I understand what you're saying, Jess. Now, if you'll excuse me, it's getting late. I think I'll go to bed."

"We haven't finished our supper," he said.

Amazed by his suggestion, she looked at him. He truly did expect her to just go on as if nothing had ever happened.

"You go ahead," she said in a voice so low he could barely hear it. "I made it for you, anyway."

She walked out of the room, her head up, her back stiff. Jess watched her until she disappeared down the hallway, then turning, he rammed his fist against the window facing.

The force ripped the skin on his knuckles, but Jess welcomed the searing pain shooting up his forearm. Maybe it would help him forget about the ache of emptiness in his heart.

Chapter Twelve

The next morning, Hannah was surprised, to say the least, when she walked into the kitchen and found Jess preparing coffee. She'd fully expected him to be at work.

"Jess," she said, pausing just inside the door, "I didn't know you were still here."

His back to her, he reached up and brought a coffee mug down from the cabinet. "I finally got a day off. I don't have to go in today."

She noticed that instead of his uniform, he was wearing blue jeans and a black rugby shirt. For a moment, her eyes clung to his broad shoulders, then moved on to his long lean legs. She remembered everything about his body, its hard, sleek muscles, its strength and warmth, the hot, sweet excitement it had given her.

At least she had that much, she thought. One night of passionate memories was more than she'd have had back in Lordsburg.

"Would you like breakfast?" she asked, her voice as casual as she could make it.

He poured himself a cup of coffee, then carried it over to the dining table. It was then that she realized he must have cleared away their uneaten supper after she'd gone to bed. The candles and wedding cake were gone, as was the wine bottle and the long-stemmed glasses. Nothing was left as a reminder of the celebration she'd prepared for them.

Poor Daniel, was all she could think. He'd worked so hard on the cake and been so proud of his effort. But he was very young, he'd soon forget. And she would, too, she supposed, after years and years had passed and she got so old that it didn't matter if Jess loved her or not. Or could she ever get that old?

"Whatever you fix for Daniel will be fine for me," he said, cutting his eyes over to where she stood just inside the room.

She was wearing a robe in some sort of silky material the deep violet blue of a concord grape. Her hair hadn't been brushed and it lay in a tangled web of curls on her shoulders. Oscar was at her feet, arching his back lovingly against her legs as though he, too, found her irresistible.

In spite of everything Jess had told her last night, he found himself wanting to go to her, wind his fingers in her tangled hair, take her mouth until she was clinging to him and he was so on fire for her that all he cared about was putting out the flames.

Hannah didn't look at him, but his voice was stiff and guarded. Maybe he expected her to burst into an angry, embarrassing tirade, she thought. Maybe he was even afraid she would go so far as to try to seduce him. Well, he needn't worry about any of those things, she thought sadly. She knew what she had to do. It was only a matter of getting herself together and doing it.

A few minutes later, Daniel appeared in the kitchen. He was delighted to find his father home and raced to climb up in his lap.

Jess kissed his son's cheek, then playfully tugged at his chin. "How's my favorite boy this morning?"

"I'm good, Daddy. I'm glad you're home."

"I am, too, sport," he said, then couldn't help but glance over to where Hannah was breaking eggs into a bowl.

I don't know what you've done to me, Jess, but I can't seem to quit chattering.

She'd looked and sounded so utterly happy at that moment, he thought, but now he doubted he'd ever hear her chatter again.

"Did you like the cake, Daddy? Hannah let me help her and she said we had to do a good job and make it pretty because it was for you."

"It was very nice," Jess told him, wondering why there was such a pain around his heart. Maybe it was because he hadn't slept at all last night, or perhaps the awful ache in his chest was because the last meal he'd had was yesterday at noon.

"Can I eat a piece now, Mommy?" Daniel asked, climbing down from his father's lap and skipping over to Hannah.

For all she knew, Jess had thrown the cake in the garbage. She lifted wounded, questioning eyes to him.

"In the pantry," he mouthed back at her.

Sighing, Hannah smiled gently at Daniel. "After breakfast, you can have a great big piece. I promise."

Later that morning when Hannah was putting clothes into the washer, Jess stuck his head in the doorway of the utility room.

Since he'd obviously avoided her since breakfast, she could only wonder why he'd sought her out now.

"Did you need something?" she asked carefully.

"Daniel and I are going over to Dwight's for a little while," he said, his eyes not quite meeting hers. "Do you want to come, too?"

He sounded as if having her along was the very last thing he wanted. And she knew he was inviting her only out of politeness, not because she was a part of the family. No, he didn't want a family. At least not a real one. And she never wanted to be anywhere she wasn't wanted.

Turning her back to him, she continued to stuff dirty clothes into the washing machine. "No. I've got several things here I need to do. You two go on."

An hour later, the telephone rang. When Hannah picked up the receiver, Tracie's concerned voice virtually shouted in her ear.

"What is going on, Hannah? Why aren't you over here with Jess and Daniel? I thought you told me yesterday that everything was wonderful."

Unexpected tears collected in her eyes. "What makes you think it isn't now?"

"Hmmph!" Tracie snorted. "Jess looks like hell and is acting even worse. The few words he's said to me were practically barked. Right now, Dwight's got him out back working on a Jeep. I hope everything goes well, otherwise, the mood Jess is in, he's liable to take a baseball bat to it."

"How long will that keep them busy?" Hannah asked thoughtfully.

"I don't know. Long enough for you to hightail it over here. I want to see if you look as bad as Jess does."

Hannah drew in a shaky breath. "I'm leaving, Tracie."

There was a long pause, then Tracie shouted even louder, "Leaving! What are you talking about? You mean leaving as in leaving Jess, leaving town? What?"

Hannah wiped at the wetness on her cheeks. She'd thought she'd used up all her tears as a child. Apparently, some of them had hidden away and saved themselves for Jess Malone. "I already have most of my things packed. I'm going to stay in a motel, I guess. Until I can find a place."

"Hannah, have you gone off your rocker? You and Jess just got married!"

Hannah squeezed her eyes shut and gripped the receiver. "I didn't say I was divorcing him. I just can't live with him."

Tracie groaned loudly. "Don't do anything—just stay put. Don't leave until—I've got to go," she said suddenly and slammed the receiver back on the hook.

Jess, who'd just walked into his friends' kitchen, stared suspiciously at Tracie. "Who were you talking to?"

Tracie let out a nervous little laugh. "Why, Jess, you sure are getting nosy these days."

Jess shot her an impatient look. "Was that my wife on the phone?" he demanded.

Tracie's eyebrows shot up. "It was. Why?"

"Because you looked as guilty as hell when I walked in the room."

Plopping down on a bar stool, Tracie said, "Could be you're the one who's feeling guilty."

Jess crossed to the cabinet and took down a glass. "I don't have anything to feel guilty about." He jammed the glass under the water dispenser on the refrigerator door, swallowed half a glass, then turned to Tracie. "What were you talking to my wife about, anyway?"

Jess couldn't believe that Hannah would discuss their personal life with anyone, not even Tracie. But he could be wrong. He'd gone out of his way to distance himself from Hannah. Maybe she felt there was no one else she could talk to. The idea tortured him.

"You keep calling her your wife," Tracie began, "but I wonder if you really have the right to call her that."

"Tracie, I think—" he started hotly, only to have Tracie wave her hand and quickly interrupt.

"Forget I said that, Jess," she pleaded. "I'm more concerned about how long you'll be able to call her your wife."

"What do you mean?" he asked, as he felt the blood drain from his face. *Don't leave until*—Tracie hadn't finished the rest. Oh God! "Is Hannah leaving?"

The stunned pain on his face had Tracie sliding off the stool and grabbing his forearm. "Jess, I don't know what's happened with you two. But don't go over there like a rampaging bull."

Jess felt as if his blood had suddenly turned to ice water. His whole body was shaking from the chill. "She *is* leaving! What did she tell you? Where—"

Tracie shook her blond head vehemently. "Do you really care, Jess? You only married her to have someone to care for Daniel."

"That's a hell of a thing to say!"

"Well, you did, didn't you?"

"No! I—" He stopped abruptly, then with a muttered curse wiped his hands over his face. He'd married Hannah because *he* wanted her in their lives. She filled up that empty hole in him that no one had ever been able to touch. She was sweet and gentle and giving. Oh, yes, he thought, his mind replaying the night they'd made love, she was the most giving woman he'd ever known. And he loved her.

He'd been fighting that fact for a long time. Maybe too long.

"I married Hannah for me!" The words had been locked inside him so long, the release of them was like an explosion. "Because I love her, damn it!"

Tracie's face was suddenly wreathed in smiles. "If that's the case, you'd better get home and do something about it."

Jess shoved the glass of water into Tracie's hands and hurried toward the back door. Tracie followed close on his heels.

"Can you keep Daniel here for me?" he asked urgently, anxious now to leave.

"Of course. And Jess—" Catching his arm, she raised on tiptoe and kissed his cheek. "Bring Hannah back over for supper. Okay?"

He gave her a hopeful little smile as he stepped out the door. "I hope to God I can, Tracie."

Hannah picked up the dried nosegay from her dresser. The pink color of the rosebuds hadn't yet faded, but some of the petals were beginning to loosen and fall away. She should probably put it in a plastic bag before she packed it away. Otherwise, there wouldn't be anything left to it.

There wasn't anything left to it, anyway, a little voice inside her mocked. There never was anything to the marriage and there never will be.

Doing her best to shake off the somber thought, she laid the dried roses atop her folded clothes. The bouquet was the only keepsake she had of her wedding day, other than the thin gold band on her finger. There were no photos to recount that time in her life. It hadn't been a picture-taking day.

"Hannah! Hannah!"

The sound of Jess's voice startled her and she jerked around, her hand flying to her mouth. What was he doing back so soon? She wasn't ready to face him. She didn't know if she'd ever be!

"In here, Jess," she called in a strained voice.

His boots echoed loudly on the hardwood floor as he hurried down the hallway. Hannah stood waiting in the middle of her bedroom, her back straight, her hands clenched behind her. When he came through the door, he took one look at her tearstained face, then at the open suitcase lying on her bed.

"What are you doing?" he asked, his voice so passive it was frightening.

Hannah was sure a crack had developed in her heart and every bit of hope, every drop of her life's blood was draining out through it. "I guess you can see I'm packing. Why? Did Tracie tell you—"

"Forget about Tracie," he snapped as he stepped farther into the room. "I want to know about this." He waved his hand at the boxes and bags scattered on the floor. "What were you going to do? Just sneak off while we were gone? Not say anything?"

Swallowing, Hannah forced herself to bravely hold his gaze. "No. I wasn't going to sneak off. I was going to tell you when—well, later today."

"Oh," he snarled mockingly. "You were going to tell me, but until then, you were going to act like everything was fine, like nothing had ever happened."

Her eyes suddenly blazed at him. "That *is* what you told me to do. Remember?"

His face blanched. "Why, Hannah? Why are you doing this? I kept hoping, thinking you were different from Michelle and my mother. I guess I was wrong. Again," he said bitterly.

Hannah normally had a placid temperament. But for the past couple of days, Jess had riled her to the point of fury. And now, to have him compare her to those two shallow women sent the blood pounding furiously through her.

"Don't ever do that! Don't ever compare me to them. You don't know me! You don't even care enough to get to know me."

"I can see, Hannah! You're leaving just like they did."

"And whose fault is that, Jess?" Anger propelling her, Hannah crossed the few steps separating them and jabbed her forefinger in his chest. "Tell me, Jess. Do you think I want to leave? Do you think it makes me happy to think of leaving Daniel? He's the only good thing I have in my life."

Her closeness and the fire in her eyes stirred him, had his hands reaching out, gathering her around the waist. "And what about me, Hannah?"

The question was softly spoken and Hannah felt some of her anger draining away. Glancing away from him, she said, "You don't want me in your life, Jess. You made that clear last night."

Desperately, she turned away from him and squeezed her burning eyes shut. "So I've decided I'm going to find a place here in Douglas. That way, I can still be close to Daniel."

To think of coming home and not finding her here, of never seeing her red hair and beautiful face, never holding her warm body close to his was like staring into a gaping black hole. If she left now, the light in his world would go out.

"You want to be close to Daniel. But not to me. Is that it?" he asked, curling his fingers around her upper arm.

Hannah had never felt as much pain as she did at this very moment. It was ripping through her, burning her throat, tying her stomach into an aching knot.

"That's not what I said. But yes, I guess so. I can't live with you anymore, Jess." She turned to him and though she knew her heart was on her face for him to see, there was nothing she could do about it. "I've changed," she whispered fiercely. "I'm not that old maid back in Lordsburg anymore. The one who was grateful for even one kind word from you."

"Hannah—"

"I've learned that I'm somebody, Jess. I'm not just a by-product of one of my mother's illicit affairs. I'm a woman with feelings and needs. I'm a woman who deserves to have a real family. I want more children and a husband that can love me the way that I love him."

"And what about Daniel?" he asked solemnly.

"Daniel deserves more, too. He needs a true family. Not just a pretend one." Her anger gone now, she gently lifted her fingers to his cheek, touched it as though it were his scarred heart. "So do you, Jess. You deserve to have a woman you can love. I hope that someday you can find her."

Suddenly, his hands were in her hair, his fingers twining tightly around the red, red curls. "I have found her," he growled, bringing his mouth down on hers.

Stunned by the unexpectedness of his kiss, Hannah grabbed on to his shirtfront and clung until he finally lifted his mouth and gazed down at her.

"I love you, Hannah. I love you with all my heart. I don't want you to leave. Not now. Not ever."

Feeling as if her legs were going to buckle, she gripped his shirt even tighter. "You think I'm going to believe that! You're crazy, Jess Malone. You can't just start kissing me and expect that to change everything. It's going to take a lot more than—"

He kissed her again, then putting his hands on her waist, he tossed her backward and onto the bed. "You're chattering, Hannah," he said, grinning down at her as he straddled her body.

"Chattering? Jess, what are you talking about?" she asked, her voice growing thicker and huskier with each button he popped on his shirt.

"I'm talking about love, my beautiful wife."

His shirt out of the way, he reached for the buttons on Hannah's blouse. When they refused to cooperate with his urgent fumbling, he simply ripped it open and tossed it back behind him.

Bemused by his actions, Hannah raised herself and peered over his shoulder. "You just threw my new blouse in the charity box," she told him.

Jess looked at her and then suddenly he laughed, then she laughed and they fell back in a tangled heap.

"Oh, Jess, I love you. Love you so much," she said when their laughter finally sobered and they lay facing each other.

"Say you'll never leave me, Hannah. Say you'll always be my wife," he urged, his big hand smoothing the hair back off her cheek.

"I'll always be your wife, Jess," she whispered, then scooting closer, "let me show you."

"I think I'm going to like this," he growled with pleasure as her fingers went to work releasing the buttons on his jeans.

"That's my sole intention," she murmured as she raised her mouth to his.

A long time later as they lay together propped against a mound of pillows, Jess said, "Tracie wants us to come over for supper. I guess we'd better let her know we'll be there and that I'm not out chasing you down somewhere.''

Her face pressed into the side of his neck, Hannah passed a hand over his chest and marveled that he would always be hers to touch, to love. ''You wouldn't have really chased me down, would you?''

''With lights and sirens blazing.''

''Jess!''

Laughing, he placed a kiss on her forehead. ''Well, I might have left the sirens off. But I would have found you and brought you home.''

Still awed by the fact that her husband really loved and wanted her, Hannah raised herself on her elbow and gazed into his handsome face. ''Jess, when did you first fall in love with me?''

His fingers trailed over the blazing curls that fell over her shoulder, then down to her soft white breasts. ''I think it was when you knocked on the door and handed me a loaf of pumpkin bread.''

Laughing with disbelief, she fell back against the pillows and stared dreamily at the ceiling. ''I fell in love with you a long time ago. When I was just a girl and you drove that black Harley of yours up and down the street and strutted around in a leather jacket.''

Surprised that her memory was so accurate, Jess said, ''You couldn't have loved me then. We were just teenagers. Besides,'' he added, his voice full of amusement, ''I never strutted.''

''Well, maybe you swaggered,'' she relented. Then, with a sigh of contentment, she leaned over him and pressed her lips to his. ''I've always loved you, Jess Malone. I always will.''

He knew that, knew it with everything inside him. And whatever had happened in the past seemed insignificant now. Hannah's love had wiped away the pain and the fear. His father had lost the woman he loved, but Jess never would. His wife wasn't Betty Malone. And she wasn't Michelle, either. She was Hannah. His life. His love.

He kissed her long and lingeringly, his hands on her hip and in her hair, then suddenly he flipped her over onto her back, giving her thigh a playful swat.

"I'm afraid if we don't get up, Tracie and Daniel are going to come walking through that door any minute now to check up on us," he said.

Groaning, Hannah levered herself up to a sitting position and looked around the messy bedroom. "What are we going to do about unpacking all this stuff?"

Jess reached for his shirt. "We're not going to unpack it. At least not until we carry it all into my bedroom first," he added with a devilish wink for her.

She smiled. "Well, at least we won't have to bother with the box that goes to charity."

"Uh . . . not quite," he said, leaning over and retrieving her blouse minus its buttons. "You might want this."

His face full of mischief, he threw it straight at Hannah's head. Squealing, she ducked the blouse, but couldn't manage to evade him.

Once again, they fell against the bed, their arms and legs tangled, their laughter filling the bedroom. It was the sound of love, and the joy of knowing tomorrow they would be together.

Epilogue

"Daddy, is that a fire truck coming to our house?" Daniel asked, looking anxiously up at his father as the wail of a siren sounded in the distance.

Jess waved his hand at the mesquite smoke boiling up from the barbecue grill. Sitting a few feet away in a pair of lawn chairs, Tracie and Hannah exchanged glances, then burst out laughing.

Deliberately ignoring the women, Jess looked down at Daniel who was tugging on his pant leg. "No, son. The fire truck isn't coming here. Everything is fine and nothing is burning."

"Not yet, you mean," Dwight said, yanking the spatula from his friend's hand. "Obviously Hannah has spoiled you with all her good cooking. You've forgotten how to grill a simple hamburger."

"I know what I'm doing," Jess told his buddy. "If you don't have a lot of smoke, you won't have any flavor."

"Smoke, yes. A blaze like this? I don't think so," Dwight said, pushing the meat to a different spot on the grill.

"Like he knows," Tracie whispered with a giggle to Hannah. "Dwight hasn't cooked since Bradley was born and that's been five months ago. If you could call opening a can of soup cooking."

"Well, Jess tried to cook when Deborah was born. Instant oatmeal for breakfast and fried bologna sandwiches for supper," Hannah said, laughing with fond remembrance. "But I loved him for trying."

Tracie smiled at Hannah. "I knew from the first day I met you that you and Jess were perfect for each other. You both just needed a little nudging. Now you've been married nearly a year, you're still madly in love with each other, and you have a beautiful new daughter to prove it."

With a sigh of utter contentment, Hannah glanced over to the playpen where both babies lay sleeping, for the moment at least.

"I never dreamed I could ever be this happy, Tracie," Hannah spoke with quiet reflection. "I thought I was going to live out the rest of my life alone. Now I have two adorable children and a wonderful husband."

"And don't forget you have two good friends and a new godson, too," the other woman reminded her.

Hannah nodded. "Believe me, Tracie, I don't ever forget how blessed I am."

Moments later, the men announced the burgers were ready and everyone sat down at a wooden picnic table to eat. Halfway through the meal, Deborah woke from her nap. Jess collected the baby from the playpen and carried her back to the table, but when she refused to quit fussing he finally handed her to Hannah.

"I guess she must be hungry, and I can't do anything about that," Jess said, gently placing the red-headed infant in his wife's arms.

"Can Deborah eat a hamburger, Mommy?" Daniel asked. "She might like it."

"I'm sure your sister will like one eventually," Hannah told him while rocking the baby back and forth in her arms. "But right now she doesn't have any teeth. She isn't big enough yet to eat a hamburger."

"Then maybe if I kissed her she would quit crying," Daniel suggested, then promptly leaned over and smacked a kiss on his sister's forehead.

The baby girl only wailed louder, making everyone at the table laugh.

"Go ahead and eat without me," Hannah told them all, while rising with the baby. "I'll be back as soon as I feed her."

Once in the house, Hannah carried Deborah to the bedroom where she sat on the edge of the bed and opened her blouse to let the baby nurse.

A moment later, Hannah felt Jess's hand on her shoulder and she lifted her face to smile at him.

"Why aren't you eating?" she asked. "Your food will get cold."

He shook his head. "I'll eat when you do," he assured her, then leaned over and brushed his forefinger against his daughter's cheek. "I don't get to see the two of you like this often enough."

"Why, Jess Malone, you act like your daughter is the most beautiful thing in the world," she teased.

Chuckling, Jess moved his finger from the baby's cheek onto Hannah's soft breast. "She is. Next to her mother."

Hannah playfully swatted his hand away. For punishment Jess bent his head and placed a seductive kiss on the side of her neck.

"Flatterer," she murmured, twisting her head to find his lips with hers.

After she'd kissed him, Jess turned his attention back to his daughter, who was still feeding hungrily at Hannah's breast. "I only wish Daniel could have had you for his mother when he was born. I was so clumsy with him."

Love surged through Hannah as she glanced up at her husband's face. "You couldn't have been clumsy. You're a wonderful father. And when our son and daughter are all grown up I'm sure they'll tell you so."

With a satisfied grunt, he folded his arms around Hannah's shoulders and pressed his cheek to hers. "So I'm a wonderful father. How am I doing in the husband department?"

Hannah laughed softly. "After our friends go home tonight, I'll put you to the test. Think you're up to it?"

His husky response was like a caress. "Only for the rest of my life."

*   *   *   *   *

Rugged and lean...and the best-looking, sweetest-talking men to be found in the entire Lone Star state!

Diana Palmer

LONG, TALL TEXANS

In July 1994, Silhouette is very proud to bring you Diana Palmer's first three LONG, TALL TEXANS. CALHOUN, JUSTIN and TYLER—the three cowboys who started the legend. Now they're back by popular demand in one classic volume—and they're ready to lasso your heart! Beautifully repackaged for this special event, this collection is sure to be a longtime keepsake!

"Diana Palmer makes a reader want to find a Texan of her own to love!"   —*Affaire de Coeur*

LONG, TALL TEXANS—the first three— reunited in this special roundup!

Available in July, wherever Silhouette books are sold.

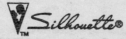

Take 4 bestselling love stories FREE

Plus get a FREE surprise gift!

Special Limited-time Offer

Mail to Silhouette Reader Service™

3010 Walden Avenue
P.O. Box 1867
Buffalo, N.Y. 14269-1867

YES! Please send me 4 free Silhouette Romance™ novels and my free surprise gift. Then send me 6 brand-new novels every month, which I will receive months before they appear in bookstores. Bill me at the low price of $2.19 each plus 25¢ delivery and applicable sales tax, if any.* That's the complete price and—compared to the cover prices of $2.75 each—quite a bargain! I understand that accepting the books and gift places me under no obligation ever to buy any books. I can always return a shipment and cancel at any time. Even if I never buy another book from Silhouette, the 4 free books and the surprise gift are mine to keep forever.

215 BPA ANRP

Name	(PLEASE PRINT)	
Address	Apt. No.	
City	State	Zip

This offer is limited to one order per household and not valid to present Silhouette Romance™ subscribers. *Terms and prices are subject to change without notice. Sales tax applicable in N.Y.

USROM-94R   ©1990 Harlequin Enterprises Limited

HE'S MORE THAN A MAN, HE'S ONE OF OUR

MAIL-ORDER BROOD
Arlene James

Leon Paradise was shocked when he discovered that his mail-order bride came with a ready-made family. No sooner had he said his vows when a half-dozen kids showed up on his doorstep. Now the handsome rancher had to decide if his home—and his heart—were big enough for Cassie Esterbridge *and* the brood she'd brought into his life.

Look for *Mail-Order Brood* by Arlene James.
Available in August.
Fall in love with our Fabulous Fathers!

R O M A N C E™

FF894

It's our 1000th Silhouette Romance™, and we're celebrating!

And to say "THANK YOU" to our wonderful readers, we would like to send you a

FREE AUSTRIAN CRYSTAL BRACELET

This special bracelet truly captures the spirit of CELEBRATION 1000! and is a stunning complement to any outfit! And it can be yours FREE just for enjoying SILHOUETTE ROMANCE™.

FREE GIFT OFFER

To receive your free gift, complete the certificate according to directions. Be certain to enclose the required number of proofs-of-purchase. Requests must be received no later than August 31, 1994. Please allow 6 to 8 weeks for receipt of order. Offer good while quantities of gifts last. Offer good in U.S. and Canada only.

And that's not all! Readers can also enter our...

CELEBRATION 1000! SWEEPSTAKES

In honor of our 1000th SILHOUETTE ROMANCE™, we'd like to award $1000 to a lucky reader!

As an added value every time you send in a completed offer certificate with the correct amount of proofs-of-purchase, your name will automatically be entered in our CELEBRATION 1000! Sweepstakes. The sweepstakes features a grand prize of $1000. PLUS, 1000 runner-up prizes of a FREE SILHOUETTE ROMANCE™, autographed by one of CELEBRATION 1000!'s special featured authors will be awarded. These volumes are sure to be cherished for years to come, a true commemorative keepsake.

DON'T MISS YOUR OPPORTUNITY TO WIN! ENTER NOW!

CELOFFER

CELEBRATION 1000! FREE GIFT OFFER

ORDER INFORMATION:

To receive your free AUSTRIAN CRYSTAL BRACELET, send three original proof-of-purchase coupons from any SILHOUETTE ROMANCE™ title published in April through July 1994 with the Free Gift Certificate completed, plus $1.75 for postage and handling (check or money order—please do not send cash) payable to Silhouette Books CELEBRATION 1000! Offer. Hurry! Quantities are limited.

FREE GIFT CERTIFICATE   096 KBM

Name:_____

Address:_____

City:_____ State/Prov.:_____ Zip/Postal:_____

Mail this certificate, three proofs-of-purchase and check or money order to CELEBRATION 1000! Offer, Silhouette Books, 3010 Walden Avenue, P.O. Box 9057, Buffalo, NY 14269-9057 or P.O. Box 622, Fort Erie, Ontario L2A 5X3. Please allow 4-6 weeks for delivery. Offer expires August 31, 1994.

PLUS

Every time you submit a completed certificate with the correct number of proofs-of-purchase, you are automatically entered in our CELEBRATION 1000! SWEEPSTAKES to win the GRAND PRIZE of $1000 CASH! PLUS, 1000 runner-up prizes of a FREE Silhouette Romance™, autographed by one of CELEBRATION 1000!'s special featured authors, will be awarded. No purchase or obligation necessary to enter. See below for alternate means of entry and how to obtain complete sweepstakes rules.

CELEBRATION 1000! SWEEPSTAKES
NO PURCHASE OR OBLIGATION NECESSARY TO ENTER

You may enter the sweepstakes without taking advantage of the CELEBRATION 1000! FREE GIFT OFFER by hand-printing on a 3" x 5" card (mechanical reproductions are not acceptable) your name and address and mailing it to: CELEBRATION 1000! Sweepstakes, P.O. Box 9057, Buffalo, NY 14269-9057 or P.O. Box 622, Fort Erie, Ontario L2A 5X3. Limit: one entry per envelope. Entries must be sent via First Class mail and be received no later than August 31, 1994. No liability is assumed for lost, late or misdirected mail.

Sweepstakes is open to residents of the U.S. (except Puerto Rico) and Canada, 18 years of age or older. All federal, state, provincial, municipal and local laws apply. Offer void wherever prohibited by law. Odds of winning dependent on the number of entries received. For complete rules, send a self-addressed, stamped envelope to: CELEBRATION 1000! Rules, P.O. Box 4200, Blair, NE 68009.

 ONE PROOF OF PURCHASE

096KBM

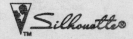